nickelodeon
THE LOUD HOUSE
3 IN 1 #4
W9-BKN-490
PAPERCUTZ
New York

MORE GREAT GRAPHIC NOVEL SERIES AVAILABLE FROM

PAPERCUTZ™

THE SMURFS TALES

BRINA THE CAT

CAT & CAT

THE SISTERS

ATTACK OF THE STUFF

LOLA'S SUPER CLUB

SCHOOL FOR EXTRATERRESTRIAL GIRLS

GERONIMO STILTON REPORTER

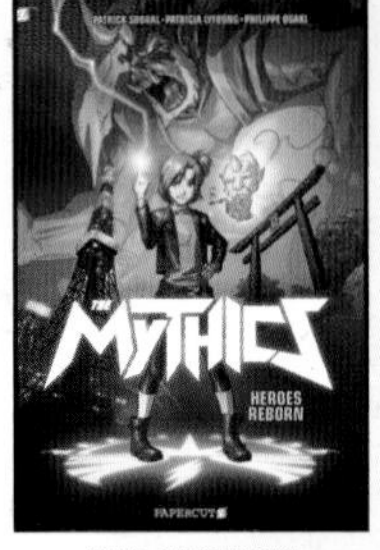

THE MYTHICS

GUMBY

MELOWY

BLUEBEARD

GILBERT

ASTERIX

FUZZY BASEBALL

THE CASAGRANDES

THE LOUD HOUSE

MANOSAURS

GEEKY F@B 5

THE ONLY LIVING GIRL

papercutz.com

Also available where ebooks are sold.

nickelodeon

3 IN 1 #4

"THE HAUNTED HOUSE"
Derek Fridolfs — Writer
Max Alley — Artist
Amanda Rynda — Colorist
Wilson Ramos Jr. — Letterer
7

"TWINNING AT LIFE"
Caitlin Fein — Writer
Agny Innocente — Artist, Colorist
Wilson Ramos Jr. — Letterer
27

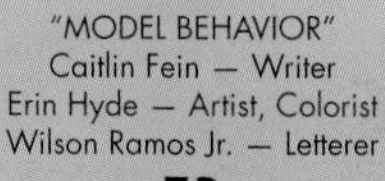

"LUCY OF MELANCHOLIA"
Caitlin Fein — Writer
Gizelle Orbino — Artist, Colorist
Wilson Ramos Jr. — Letterer
10

"MODEL BEHAVIOR"
Caitlin Fein — Writer
Erin Hyde — Artist, Colorist
Wilson Ramos Jr. — Letterer
32

"ROCKIN' ROUTINE"
Kiernan Sjursen-Lien — Writer
Lee-Roy Lahey — Artist
Hallie Lal — Colorist
Wilson Ramos Jr. — Letterer
14

"TERMS OF ENDEARMENT"
Jared Morgan — Writer, Artist, Colorist, Letterer
38

"NONE CHUCKED"
Derek Fridolfs, Zazo Aguiar — Writers
Zazo Aguiar — Artist, Colorist
Wilson Ramos Jr. — Letterer
15

"BRACE FOR IT"
Derek Fridolfs — Writer
Kelsey Wooley — Artist, Colorist
Wilson Ramos Jr. — Letterer
44

"BIG GAINS"
Jared Morgan — Writer, Artist, Colorist, Letterer
21

"CANDY HUNTING AT HUNTINGTON MANOR"
Sammie Crowley — Writer
Ari Castleton — Artist
Gabrielle Dolbey — Colorist
Wilson Ramos Jr. — Letterer
46

TODD OMAN — Cover Artist
JAMES SALERNO — Sr. Art Director/Nickelodeon
JAYJAY JACKSON — Design
SAMMIE CROWLEY, SEAN GANTKA, ANGELA ENTZMINGER, ASHLEY KLIMENT, AMANDA RYNDA, JARED MORGAN, CAITLIN FEIN, KEVIN SULLIVAN, SONIA CANO, EMMA BONE, CAITLIN FEIN, KRISTEN G. SMITH, NEIL WADE, DANA CLUVERIUS, MOLLIE FREILICH — Special Thanks
JEFF WHITMAN — Editor
INGRID RIOS — Editorial Intern
JOAN HILTY — Comics Editor/Nickelodeon
JIM SALICRUP
Editor-in-Chief

ISBN: 978-1-5458-0639-5

Papercutz books may be purchased for business or promotional use. For information on bulk purchases please contact Macmillan Corporate and Premium Sales Department at (800) 221-7945 x5442.

Printed in Canada
December 2021

Distributed by Macmillan
Third Printing

"I KNOW WHERE YOU SHOPPED LAST SUMMER"
Caitlin Fein — Writer
Ron Bradley — Artist, Colorist
Wilson Ramos Jr. — Letterer
60

"HOME SICKNESS"
Kiernan Sjursen-Lien — Writer
Jose Hernandez — Artist, Colorist
Wilson Ramos Jr. — Letterer
64

"MUSICAL MYRTLE"
Jair Holguin, George Holguin — Writers
George Holguin — Artist, Colorist
Wilson Ramos Jr. — Letterer
65

"OCEAN 11"
Derek Fridolfs — Writer
Tyler Koberstein — Artist, Colorist
Wilson Ramos Jr. — Letterer
68

"FREE TO BE ME"
Kiernan Sjursen-Lien — Writer
Zazo Aguiar — Artist, Colorist
Wilson Ramos Jr. — Letterer
71

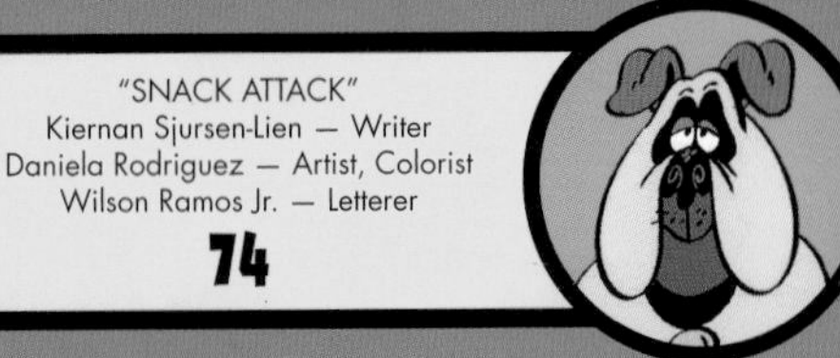

"SNACK ATTACK"
Kiernan Sjursen-Lien — Writer
Daniela Rodriguez — Artist, Colorist
Wilson Ramos Jr. — Letterer
74

"THAT'S A WRAP"
Ron Bradley — Writer, Artist, Colorist
Wilson Ramos Jr. — Letterer
78

"MACABRE MUNCHIES"
Kiernan Sjursen-Lien — Writer
Tyler Koberstein — Artist, Colorist
Wilson Ramos Jr. — Letterer
79

"CANNONBALL RUN"
Jair Holguin, George Holguin — Writers
George Holguin — Artist
Ronda Pattison — Colorist
Wilson Ramos Jr. — Letterer
81

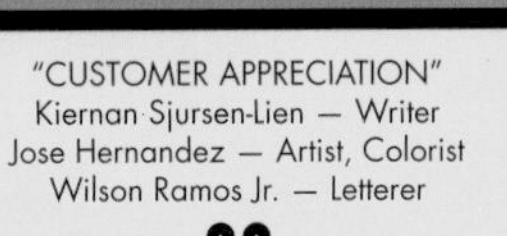

"CUSTOMER APPRECIATION"
Kiernan Sjursen-Lien — Writer
Jose Hernandez — Artist, Colorist
Wilson Ramos Jr. — Letterer
88

"ROBOT RUMPUS"
Kiernan Sjursen-Lien — Writer
Melissa Kleynowski — Artist
Princess Bizares— Colorist
Wilson Ramos Jr. — Letterer
89

"HOOK, LINE, AND STINKER"
Jared Morgan — Writer, Artist,
Colorist, Letterer
92

"ONE, TWO, SWITCHEROO"
Kiernan Sjursen-Lien — Writer
Max Alley — Artist
Peter Bertucci —Colorist
Wilson Ramos Jr. — Letterer
98

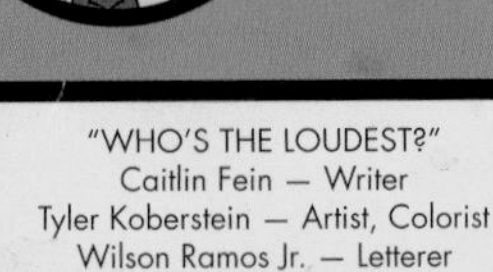

"WHO'S THE LOUDEST?"
Caitlin Fein — Writer
Tyler Koberstein — Artist, Colorist
Wilson Ramos Jr. — Letterer
101

"THE CASE OF THE STOLEN DRAWERS"
Kiernan Sjursen-Lien — Writer
Tyler Koberstein — Artist, Colorist
Wilson Ramos Jr. — Letterer
108

"GOING COCO-NUTS!"
Jair Holguin — Writer
Erin Hunting — Artist, Colorist
Wilson Ramos Jr. — Letterer
114

"OLLIE OLLIE OXEN FREE"
Jair Holguin — Writer
Zazo Aguiar — Artist, Colorist
Vic Miyuki — Colorist
Wilson Ramos Jr. — Letterer
118

"TONGUE TIED"
Julia Guillen — Writer
Ron Bradley — Artist, Colorist
Wilson Ramos Jr. — Letterer
123

"ZACH AND THE MEAN CHALK"
Derek Fridolfs — Writer
Erin Hyde — Artist, Colorist
Wilson Ramos Jr. — Letterer
129

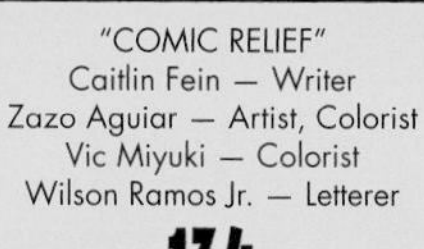

"COMIC RELIEF"
Caitlin Fein — Writer
Zazo Aguiar — Artist, Colorist
Vic Miyuki — Colorist
Wilson Ramos Jr. — Letterer
134

"LEVEL UP"
Kiernan Sjursen-Lien — Writer
Lee-Roy Lahey — Artist
Peter Bertucci — Colorist
Wilson Ramos Jr. — Letterer
139

"MEAT YOUR MAKER"
Derek Fridolfs — Writer
George Holguin — Artist
Vic Miyuki — Colorist
Wilson Ramos Jr. — Letterer
143

"MODEL PETS"
Kacey Wooley-Huang — Writer
Kelsey Wooley — Artist, Colorist
Wilson Ramos Jr. — Letterer
147

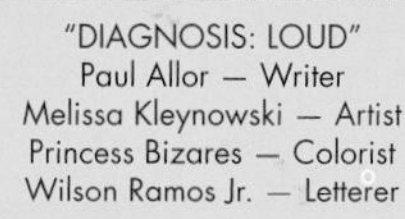

"DIAGNOSIS: LOUD"
Paul Allor — Writer
Melissa Kleynowski — Artist
Princess Bizares — Colorist
Wilson Ramos Jr. — Letterer
152

"CAKE-NSTEIN'S MONSTER"
Paul Allor — Writer
Erin Hunting — Artist, Colorist
Wilson Ramos Jr. — Letterer
155

THE LOUD HOUSE #10 Cover Art by COLTON DAVIS

"THE HAUNTED HOUSE"

KLINK BANG RATTLE-RATTLE
THERE IT IS AGAIN. FOLLOW THOSE SOUNDS!

RINGGGG
IT'S COMING FROM UP THERE. YOU LOOK FIRST!
GULP! THINK IT'S AN ALIEN ABDUCTION?

THAT OR GULP! WE ARE BEING HAUNTED BY GREGORY FARFUNKEL!*
SHUDDER
*SEE THE LOUD HOUSE #5 "AFTER DARK" FOR THE CHILLING TALE.

EEEEEEEK!
CLICK
RINGGGG

EEEEEEK!

OH, IT'S ONLY YOU TWO. THANKS FOR FINDING ME.
DAD, WHAT ARE YOU DOING UP HERE?

I'VE BEEN STUCK IN THIS ATTIC ALL EVENING. JUST TRYING TO FIND MY COLLECTION OF PRIZED COW BELLS.

IT APPEARS YOUR HOUSE ISN'T HAUNTED AFTER ALL.
RATTLE RATTLE
1
3
OLD TOYS

IT ALSO APPEARS THAT WE'RE NOW **STUCK.**
HEY! LET US *OUUUUUT!*
WUMPH
WUMPH
WUMPH

WUMPH WUMPH WUMPH
OOOO... DID YOU HEAR THAT? I THINK OUR HOUSE IS HAUNTED.
YOU KNOW WHAT THAT MEANS? IT'S GHOST HUNTING TIME!
BEST. NIGHT. EVER.

END?

"LUCY OF MELANCHOLIA"

GRISELDA?
AND GRISELDA?

AND GRISELDA?

AW, NOTHING LIKE A QUIET NIGHT IN WITH MY FAVORITE TV SHOW: "VAMPIRES OF MELANCHOLIA."
EDWIN, IT'S NOT WHAT YOU THINK. I'M CURSED WITH A DEVASTATING SECRET. THE SECRET IS--
THE BURPIN' BURGER!

JEAN JUAN'S!
THE BURPIN' BURGER!

SIGH. I THOUGHT YOU WERE ALL GOING OUT TONIGHT?

CHILLAX, WE'RE LEAVING...

...ONCE THEY COME TO THEIR SENSES.
COME ON, DUDES!
YOU NEVER GO WITH MY PICK!
I NEED MY PROTEIN!
SIGH.

IT'S NOT EASY FOR A MODERN GOTH GIRL TO LIVE WITH SUCH A LIVELY FAMILY.

YAWN! I WISH I LIVED SOMEWHERE DARK AND QUIET. SOMEWHERE LIKE.... LIKE...

ZZZZ.

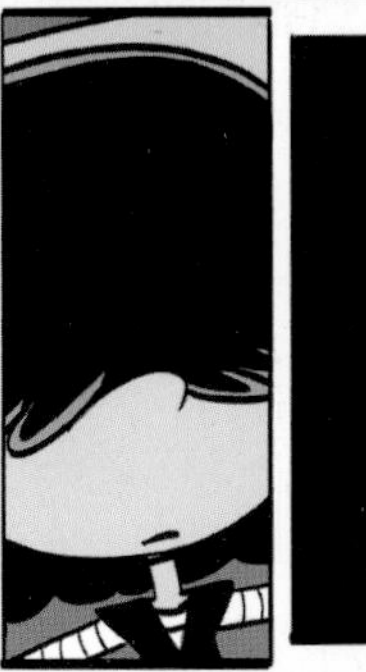

LUCINDA! THE SUN SETS. IT'S TIME TO RISE.

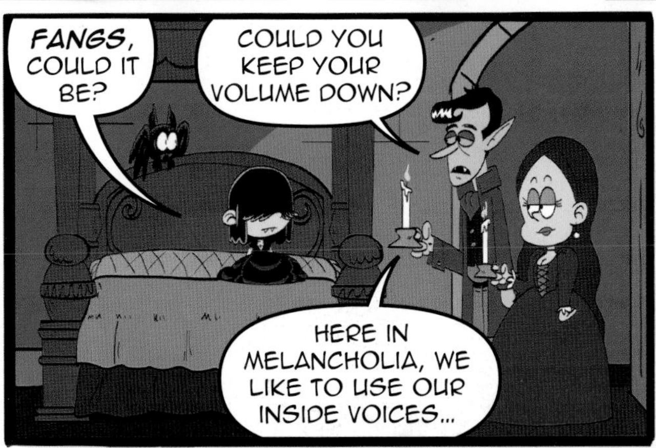
FANGS, COULD IT BE?
COULD YOU KEEP YOUR VOLUME DOWN?
HERE IN MELANCHOLIA, WE LIKE TO USE OUR INSIDE VOICES...

I'M HOME.

THIS BOOK IS EVERYTHING.
Modern Embalming Practices
SSSSH.
SHHHHH.

UM, SORRY...
SHHHHH.

CAW!
SHHHHH.

COUGH!
DID YOU SAY SOMETHING?

SHAKE

SIGH. ALL THE GARLIC-FREE GARLIC BREAD IN THE WORLD COULDN'T LIVEN UP THIS DINNER...

FANGS, I NEVER THOUGHT I'D SAY THIS BUT...I WISH I WAS SOMEWHERE **LOUDER.**
YAWN!

YAWN! I COULDN'T SAY IT BETTER MYSELF.
SNORE!

CAW! LUCY. LUCY, WAKE UP!

LUCY?
HUH?

YO, WAKE UP! WE FINALLY PICKED A PLACE.

THE BURPIN' BURGER!
JEAN JUAN'S!

AND YOU WANT ME TO GO WITH YOU?

YUP!
ONLY IF YOU'RE QUICK ABOUT IT!
LET'S GO! I'M HUNGRY!
DUH, LITTLE DUDE!

I GUESS IT'S NICE TO HAVE THINGS A LITTLE LIVELY.
LYNN! GET OFF OF MY SHOULDERS!

SOMETIMES.
END

"ROCKIN' ROUTINE"

"NONE CHUCKED"

DROP
POOF
COUGH. NINJAS, OF COURSE.
THOSE ARE COOL OUTFITS!
YOU REALLY THINK SO? YOU'VE GOT GREAT TASTE. I DESIGNED THEM MYSELF!
WHAT?! DON'T COMPLIMENT THE ENEMY!
SORRY, ACE.

DO ME A FAVOR. JUST KEEP THIS BOOK OUT OF THEIR HANDS.
WAIT!
I'VE GOT BAD DEPTH PERCEPTION!
BONK
HOME RUN!
HEY, GIVE THAT BACK! IT DOESN'T BELONG TO YOU!
SOME KIND OF BOOK WRITTEN IN SOME WEIRD SECRET CODE.
THAT'S JAPANESE, DEAR SISTER. ALLOW ME TO DECIPHER THE SECRET ART OF THE NINJA.
IT'S NINJA TIME!

LISA NOW MAKES MORE SMOKE BOMBS THAN EVER BEFORE. LILY'S STINK BOMBS ARE TEN TIMES MORE LETHAL.
LENI CHANNELED HER INNER VISION FOR NINJA-WEAR, WITH HER PROWESS, SHE CAN MAKE NINJA OUTFITS OUT OF ANYTHING.
I RAN OUT OF LUCY'S BED SPREAD.
LUNA GAINED THE POWER OF FURIOUS SOUND. THIS NINJA CAN MAKE SOME REAL NOISE.
I'M THE SHREDDER!
LYNN GOT A SUPREME TECHNIQUE FOR EXTRA-SPORTY NINJA EQUIPMENT!
LUAN LEARNED THE SACRED ART OF THE INFINITE KNOCK KNOCK JOKE. THEY KEEP KNOCKING, BUT YOU WILL NEVER LEARN WHO'S THERE...
LOLA AND LANA MASTERED THE ELEMENTS OF THE EARTH AND THE STARS.
BE IT GLITTER OR DIRT, THESE TWO KNOW HOW TO GET EVERYWHERE.
AND ME, I WAS ALWAYS AWESOME, SO WHY CHANGE LITERAL PERFECTION.

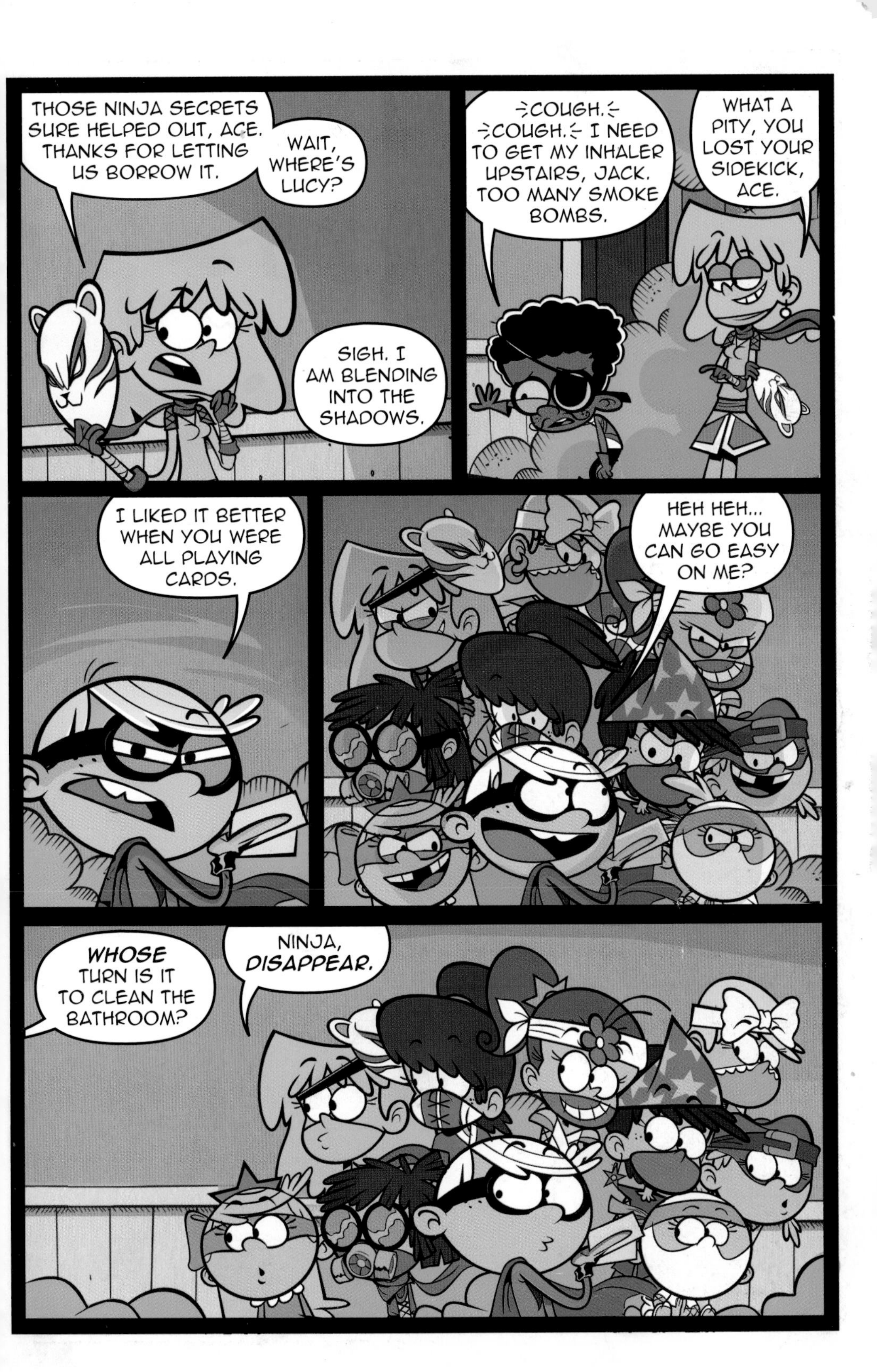
THOSE NINJA SECRETS SURE HELPED OUT, ACE. THANKS FOR LETTING US BORROW IT.
WAIT, WHERE'S LUCY?
SIGH. I AM BLENDING INTO THE SHADOWS.
COUGH. *COUGH.* I NEED TO GET MY INHALER UPSTAIRS, JACK. TOO MANY SMOKE BOMBS.
WHAT A PITY, YOU LOST YOUR SIDEKICK, ACE.
I LIKED IT BETTER WHEN YOU WERE ALL PLAYING CARDS.
HEH HEH... MAYBE YOU CAN GO EASY ON ME?
WHOSE TURN IS IT TO CLEAN THE BATHROOM?
NINJA, DISAPPEAR.

BANNFF
ACE, I GOT THE BOOK BACK FROM LILY. IT'S KIND OF GROSS.
ALL TOO LATE, JACK. THEY WON.
BUT AT LEAST YOU CAN HELP ME WITH MY CHORES, HUH, BUDDY?
SORRY, PAL. I'M ALLERGIC TO CLEANING PRODUCTS.
WELL, I'LL SEE MYSELF OUT. NEXT TIME, LET'S PLAY NINJA AT MY PLACE.
IT WAS LUCY'S TURN TO CLEAN THE BATHROOM TOO.
SHE COULD'VE AT LEAST GAVE ME A HAND HERE... HMPF! NINJAS...
SHH!
END

big gains

TODAY I'M HELPING LYNN WITH HER WORKOUT ROUTINE LEADING UP TO A BIG WRESTLING MATCH.

FIRST THOUGH, I'M MAKING HER SPECIAL PRE-WORKOUT SMOOTHIE!
WHIRRRR

ALRIGHT, LYNN! I'VE GOT YOUR SPECIAL PRE-WORKOUT SMOOTHIE ALL BLENDED UP AND READY TO GO!
SNATCH
GLUG GLUG
-BURP- YEAH! LET'S GET THIS WORKOUT STARTED!
THAT'S THE SPIRIT!

ALRIGHT, LINCOLN. WHAT'S UP FIRST?
LET'S SEE, UP FIRST IS--
SOME BABY DUMBBELLS? TOO EASY. I'M GONNA NEED SOME MORE WEIGHT IF I'M GONNA BUILD MORE MUSCLE.
OH, WE'RE JUST GETTING STARTED!
C'MON! I STILL NEED MORE WEIGHT!
OOOOKAY. I THINK I HAVE AN IDEA.
MORE WEIGHT!
ALRIGHT, I THINK I HAVE *ANOTHER* IDEA.

OKAY, LYNN, I THINK THIS WORKOUT MIGHT PROVE TO BE MORE THAN A CHALLENGE.
MORE WEIGHT!

LATER...
THE LYNN-SANITY CONTINUES! WHAT ELSE YOU GOT FOR ME, LINCOLN?!
UH, I HATE TO BREAK IT TO YOU, LYNN, BUT WE BURNED THROUGH MY WORKOUT PLANS AND THEN SOME!
HUH?
HOW AM I GONNA BULK UP IF I DON'T HAVE ANY MORE WEIGHT?!
I NEED MORE WEIGHT!
?
3

?!
FOLLOW ME!
ZIP

LENI, WHAT GIVES?!

HERE YA GO!
PLOP

UGH! WHY'D YOU DRAG ME UP TO THE BATHROOM LINE?

HAHA
HAHA
I THOUGHT YOU SAID YOU WANTED-- "MORE WAIT?"

END

"TWINNING AT LIFE"

ROYAL WOODS WELCOMES TWINS!
WHOA! **LOLS**, CAN YOU BELIEVE HOW MANY PEOPLE SHOWED UP TO THE TWIN CONVENTION?
AND ALL WEARING MATCHING OUTFITS, **LANS?** TWO WORDS: NO THANKS.
OOH, GIRLS, SHOULD WE GO TO THE LECTURE ON ***TWIN TELEPATHY?*** OR ***DECONSTRUCTING DOPPLEGANGERS?***
UMMM...
WAIT! IT'S **SARA** AND **TARA** FROM MY FAVORITE SITCOM... ***"HERE COMES DOUBLE!"***

OMGOSH!
OH, GREAT. MOM'S TURNING INTO **LENI!**

WANNA DIG THROUGH THIS BAD BOY? SEE IF THERE'S ANYTHING COOL?
SIGN UP NOW FOR THE CROWN JEWEL OF THE CONVENTION: THE "TWINSIEST TWIN COMPETITION"...
THERE! THAT! COOL!

NO WAY! I DON'T WANT OUR TWIN THING TO BE JUDGED!
PLEEEEESE? I'LL MAKE YOU A MUD PIE.

UGH, MY TIGHTS ARE RIDING UP. WHY COULDN'T WE WEAR MATCHING SWEATS? OR OOH! TRACK SUITS!
GIFT SHOP
PLEASE, THE JUDGES ARE GONNA EAT THIS LOOK UP. NOW TO PRACTICE THE HARD PART.
HARD PART?
HUH. MAYBE THERE IS NO HARD PART.
RIGHT? THIS TWIN THING IS TOTALLY NATURAL!
SLURP
SLURP
IYAY AVEHAY AINBRAY EEZEFRAY!
OH, NO! IT'S FINALLY HAPPENING. MUD BRAIN! DON'T LOOK INTO THE LIGHT.
NO, SILLY! I'M TRYING TO FORM OUR OWN SPECIAL TWIN LANGUAGE! DUH!
OH. WHAT'S TWIN FOR "YOU GOT SODA ON YOUR DRESS"?
ATTENTION TWINS! THE COMPETITION IS ABOUT TO START!
WHAT?!
THERE YOU TWO ARE! WHAT ARE YOU WEARING?
IT'S SHOWTIME!
HEY!
SPLASH

THANKS, SIS.
MMM. HMM. YOU TWO WANT TO TELL ME WHAT'S GOING ON?

OH, MOM... SIGH.

WE WANT TO WIN THE TWINSIEST TWIN COMPETITION.

WE'RE SPEAKING IN UNISON!

GIRLS, THAT'S GREAT, AND QUITE FRANKLY A LITTLE UNNERVING BUT... YOU TWO SHOULDN'T TRY TO SEEM MORE ALIKE SO THAT YOU WIN A COMPETITION!

YOU SHOULD BE PROUD OF YOUR SIMILARITIES AND DIFFERENCES! YOU MAY SHARE SOME FEATURES, BUT THERE'S ONLY ONE LANA AND ONE LOLA! AND THAT'S PRETTY SPECIAL AS IS.
YOU'RE RIGHT, MOM. READY TO COMPETE AS OURSELVES, LOLS?
YEAH. LET'S WIN THIS!

ARE YOU READY TO ANNOUNCE THE CUTEST, TWINSIEST PAIR, SARA?

CAN IT BE US, TARA?!

HAHAHAHA!
GRRR! JUST PICK SOMEONE!

TARA AND SARA STILL GOT IT!
LOLA, SHH!

AND THE WINNER IS...

MOOCHIE AND MARLEY!
ARF! ARF!

GRRRR
EEK!

WELL, WE MAY NOT BE THE "TWINSIEST TWINS" BUT WE'RE NOT LEAVING EMPTY-HANDED.
YOU GOT THAT RIGHT!

WHERE DID YOU EVEN GET THAT?!

SERIOUSLY, HOW ARE WE EVEN RELATED?
TARA! SARA! CAN YOU SIGN MY SCRUNCHIE?
NOM
NOM
NOM
END

"MODEL BEHAVIOR"

HI, MIGUEL, FIONA. IS LENI OFF YET?

THIS LOOK IS SO YOU, MR. GROUSE! BUT I THINK IT'S FACING THE WRONG WAY.
HUMPH. THEN WHY CALL IT A FANNY PACK?
CHECK OUT

SHE'LL BE DONE IN FIVE.
ARE YOU HERE FOR YOUR SISTER SHOPPING DAY?
NOPE. I'M HERE FOR OUR SUPER SISTER SHOPPING DAY!

CUTE...
RIGHT?! WE HAVE SO MUCH PLANNED SINCE WE NEVER GET "JUST US" TIME AND--
I LITERALLY HAVE TO GET BOBBY THAT SWEATER!

PERF! MANNEQUIN DRESSED.
WE'VE EARNED OUR SMOOTHIE BREAK.

HEY, GIRL, LORI'S HERE!
DID YOU HEAR THAT, MR. GROUSE? IT'S TIME FOR SUPER SISTER SHOPPING DAY!
SUPER.

LORI?
LORI?!

GASP!

AAH! YOU'VE BEEN TURNED INTO A MANNEQUIN! I ALWAYS FEARED THIS DAY WOULD COME...
OH, WELL! AT LEAST, WE CAN STILL HAVE OUR MALL DAY.

DON'T YOU JUST LOVE THE HAND MASSAGE PART, LORI?

LIKE, I CAN'T WATCH!

WHICH DO YOU LIKE BETTER? CHERRY TERRIER OR SNICKERPOODLE?

CLONK

OMGOSH! I'M ALSO FALLING FOR BOTH! BEST SISTER DAY EVER!

WORST SISTER DAY EVER. I LITERALLY CAN'T FIND LENI!
REINI

OH-TO-THE-NO!
LET'S MOVE!
SPLURT!
SPLURT!

THIS IS THE FINEST WORK I'VE EVER SEEN! YOU'RE NOW HEAD MANICURIST!

GRRR. TEENS AND THEIR HAIR EXTENSIONS!

IT'S NO USE. WE'VE LOOKED EVERYWHERE WE PLANNED TO GO TO!
AND LENI'S NOT RESPONDING TO ANY OF MY CALLS OR TEXTS!

WAIT! LENI JUST POSTED A PHOTO!

@NAME:LENILOUD
CARLOTTA LIKES THIS
BEST SHOPPING DAY EVER #SUPERSISTER
THAT MANNEQUIN LITERALLY LOOKS JUST LIKE ME!
I'M REALLY NOT SURPRISED.
SLURP
BUT WHERE ARE THEY NOW?!
YOU TALKING ABOUT THAT BLONDE GIRL AND HER QUIET FRIEND?
SHE'S A MANNEQUIN.
I'M NOT HERE TO JUDGE, BUT I THINK THEY WERE HEADED TO THE PARKING LOT.

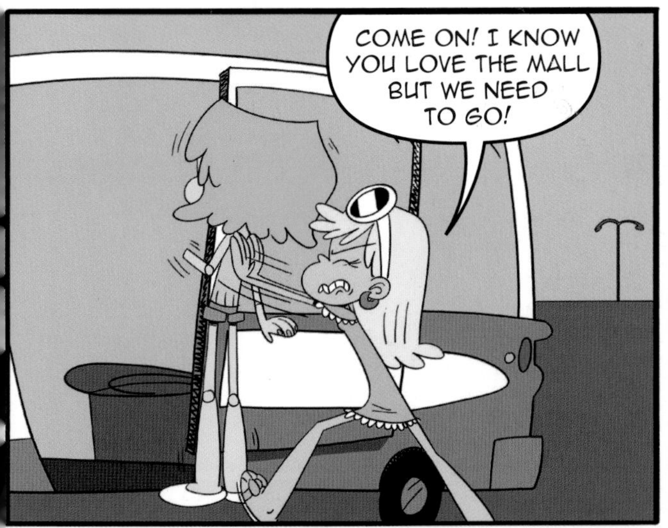
COME ON! I KNOW YOU LOVE THE MALL BUT WE NEED TO GO!

POP

OH, NO! FIRST YOUR HAND AND NOW THIS?
LORI, I DON'T KNOW WHAT TYPE OF MALL WITCH CURSED YOU BUT I VOW TO FIND OUT!
UM, LENI?

LORI? IS THAT YOU?
LIKE, YOU BET, SIS.
OH, I GET WHAT HAPPENED!

YOU HAVE A SECRET MANNEQUIN TWIN!

EEK!
CLONK
END

terms of endearment

MAIL
DING
DONG
OH, MAN! OH, MAN! IT'S HERE! IT'S FINALLY HERE!

YES!

CLYDE! COME IN
CLYDE!
ZIP
GASP!

CLYDE HERE. WHAT'S UP, LINCOLN!
IT'S HERE!

I'M ON MY WAY!

SOON...
AND NOW TIME FOR THE GRAND UNBOXING!

RIP
OPEN
PLUNGE
WHOOOOOOAAAAA!
AFTER 6 MONTHS OF WAITING, *TURBO FISH BRAWLER E.X. ALPHA 4: MODERN AQUATIC COMBAT* IS HERE!
MEGA CONSOLE 128
TURBO FISH BRAWLER EX ALPHA 4
MODERN AQUATIC COMBAT

I'VE BEEN DREAMING OF THIS DAY FOR SO LONG!
IT'S... IT'S SO BEAUTIFUL!
ZIP
WE'VE WAITED LONG ENOUGH, LET'S POP IT IN AND PLAY!
TURBO 4
TSH BRAWLER
EX ALPHA
LOADING....

PRESS START

ALRIGHT! LET'S DO THIS!

TERMS AND CONDITIONS

HUH? "TERMS AND CONDITIONS"? UH, I THINK WE CAN JUST SKIP THIS PART--

NOOOOOOOOOO!
LINCOLN! TERMS AND CONDITIONS ARE A VERY IMPORTANT PART OF LIVING IN THE DIGITAL AGE. YOU SHOULD ALWAYS CAREFULLY READ OVER WHATEVER USER AGREEMENTS YOU ENTER INTO. IT'S THE RESPONSIBLE THING TO DO!
AND BESIDES, READING IS FUN.

HRMMM.
WELL, OKAY. I GUESS THAT SOUNDS FINE.
THAT'S THE SPIRIT, LINCOLN!

TERMS AND CONDITIONS
NOW, LET'S SEE--PAGE ONE...

MUCH LATER

ALRIGHT, THIS IS ALL SOUNDING PRETTY GOOD SO FAR. ONTO PAGE 79!

MUCH MUCH LATER

ZZZZzzzz!
AND THAT CONCLUDES CLAUSE 241. WELP, THIS ALL SEEMS PRETTY STANDARD. NOW LETS GET TO THE ACTUAL GAME!

!!!
BEEP
BEEP
BEEP
BEEP

WELL, I GOTTA GO! MY DADS ONLY ALLOW ME *THIRTY MINUTES* OF VIDEO GAMES PER DAY!
BEEP BEEP
FISH BRAWLER 4
EX ALPHA
MODERN AQUATIC COMBAT
-PRESS START-

END

"BRACE FOR IT"

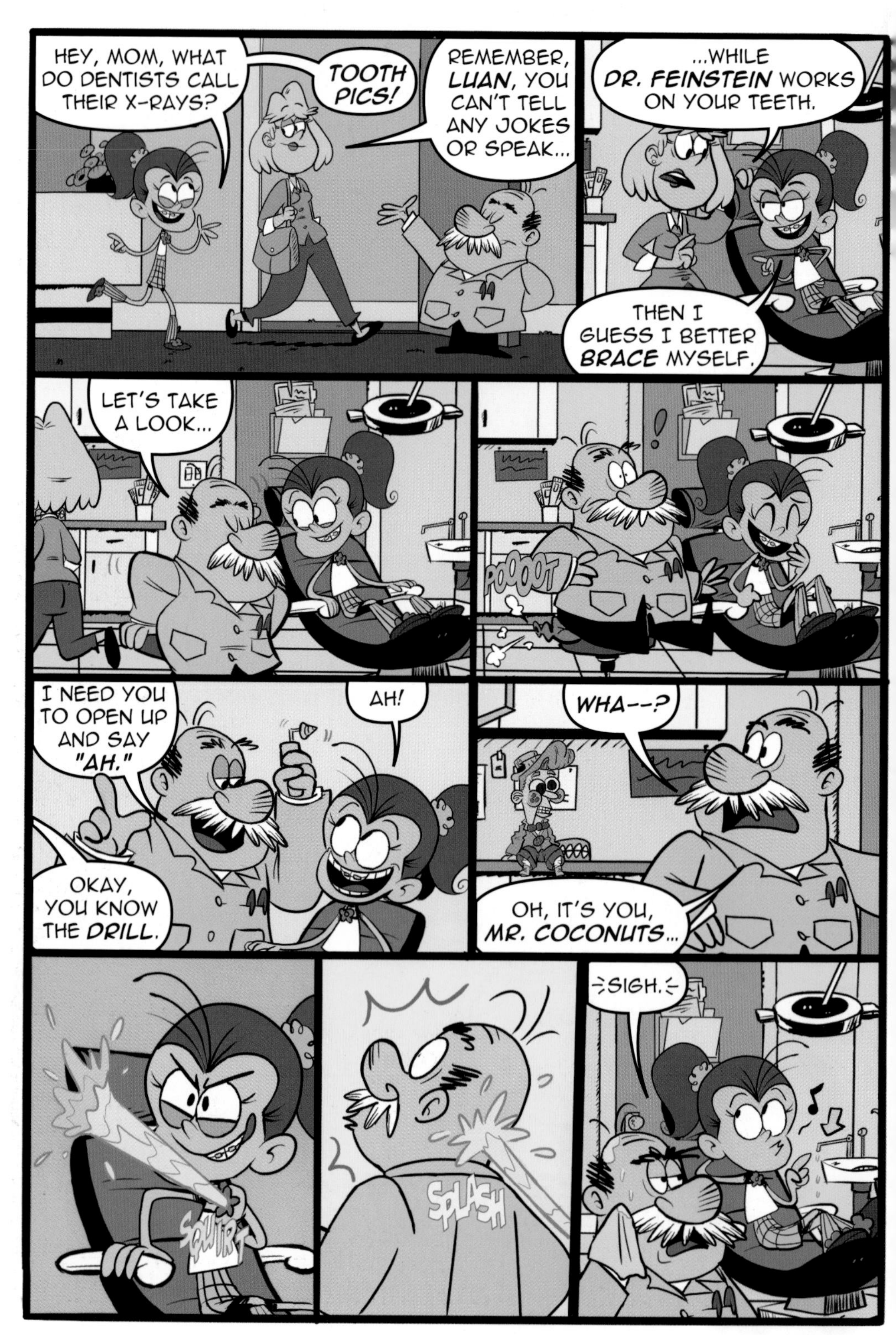
HEY, MOM, WHAT DO DENTISTS CALL THEIR X-RAYS?
TOOTH PICS!
REMEMBER, LUAN, YOU CAN'T TELL ANY JOKES OR SPEAK...
...WHILE DR. FEINSTEIN WORKS ON YOUR TEETH.
THEN I GUESS I BETTER BRACE MYSELF.
LET'S TAKE A LOOK...
POOOOT
I NEED YOU TO OPEN UP AND SAY "AH."
AH!
OKAY, YOU KNOW THE DRILL.
WHA--?
OH, IT'S YOU, MR. COCONUTS...
SQUIRT
SPLASH
SIGH.

YOUR DAUGHTER IS QUITE THE COMEDIAN, RITA.
SHE'S THE ONLY PATIENT TO TEST MY GAG REACTION.
CHATTER CHATTER
ARF ARFFF I AM THE WALRUS!
CLAP CLAP
THAT'S ENOUGH, LUAN...
SQUIRT
KA-SNORT
HOW DID YOUR DENTIST APPOINTMENT GO?
I GOT A STANDING OVATION.
MY STAND-UP ROUTINE IS EVEN BETTER SITTING DOWN!
NEXT DAY OFF, I AM STAYING OUT OF THE OFFICE.
END

"CANDY HUNTING AT HUNTINGTON MANOR"

KNOCK
KNOCK
KNOCK

TRICK OR TREAT!

WHAT LOVELY COSTUMES!

BITE-SIZED CANDY?!
WHAT HAPPENED TO THIS PLACE, *LINC?!* WHERE ARE THE FULL-SIZE BARS?

KEEP IN MIND, THESE ARE MY *SAMPLE* SIZES.

ONCE YOU PICK A FAVORITE, I'LL GIVE YOU THE *FULL-SIZED* VERSION!
FULL
SIZE

"SNAG"

NOM
NOM

WE'LL TAKE ONE OF EACH!

I HOPE THEY DON'T THINK WE'RE TOO *OLD* TO BE TRICK-OR-TREATING, *LENI*...

DING DONG

OH, I SEE WE HAVE SOME "TEENS" OUT TONIGHT.

HEH. HEH.

TAKE *EXTRA!* YOU'RE GROWING!

OKAY, NOW DON'T FORGET, LANA...WE HAVE ANOTHER SET OF COSTUMES TO CHANGE INTO IF WE DON'T GET ENOUGH OUT OF THIS HOUSE.
DING DONG

TRICK OR TREAT!

WOOSH

I DON'T THINK WE'RE GOING TO BE NEEDING OUR COSTUME CHANGES, LOLA...

SICK DUDS, DUDE!
PUNS DON'T GET CANDY. PUNS DON'T GET CANDY.

TRICK OR TREAT!

WOOSH

DROOL

OKAY, SO IF THEY DON'T COUGH UP THE GOOD STUFF... YOU SCARE 'EM INTO GIVING IT UP, LUCY!
KNOCK KNOCK

TRICK OR TREAT!

THANKS!

OKAY, LILY, LET'S MAKE SURE WE'RE PUTTING OUT MAXIMUM CUTENESS FOR MAXIMUM CANDY RETURN!
GOO!

DING DONG

TRICK OR TREAT!
ICK AME!

NAB
ON

CANDY BLASTER 5000

BEEP
BEEP

CLICK
ON

FOOSH

CLICK

WELL, THIS TURNED OUT EVEN BETTER THAN I POSSIBLY COULD HAVE HYPOTHESIZED.

♫ WHO'S THE BEST? ♫
CLINCOLN McCLYDE!
♫ WHO GOT THE CANDY?
CLINCOLN McCLYDE!
♫ UH-HUH! OH, YEAH! THAT'S ♫ RIGHT! ♫
HA!
HA!
HA!

WHAP
SOC
BIFF

AHEM!

ARE YOU BOYS DONE YET? WE SHOULD ***PROBABLY*** GO HOME...

YOU'RE RIGHT, ***LORI,*** WE PROBABLY HAVE ENOUGH CANDY.

WHAT DID I TELL YOU GUYS? THIS PLACE IS AMAZING, RIGHT?!
GNARLY!
WE SHOULD HAVE ENOUGH CANDY TO LAST US UNTIL NEXT HALLOWEEN! OR...YOU KNOW, AT LEAST UNTIL THANKSGIVING.
TRICK OR TREAT
RIP
END

THE
LOUD
HOUSE

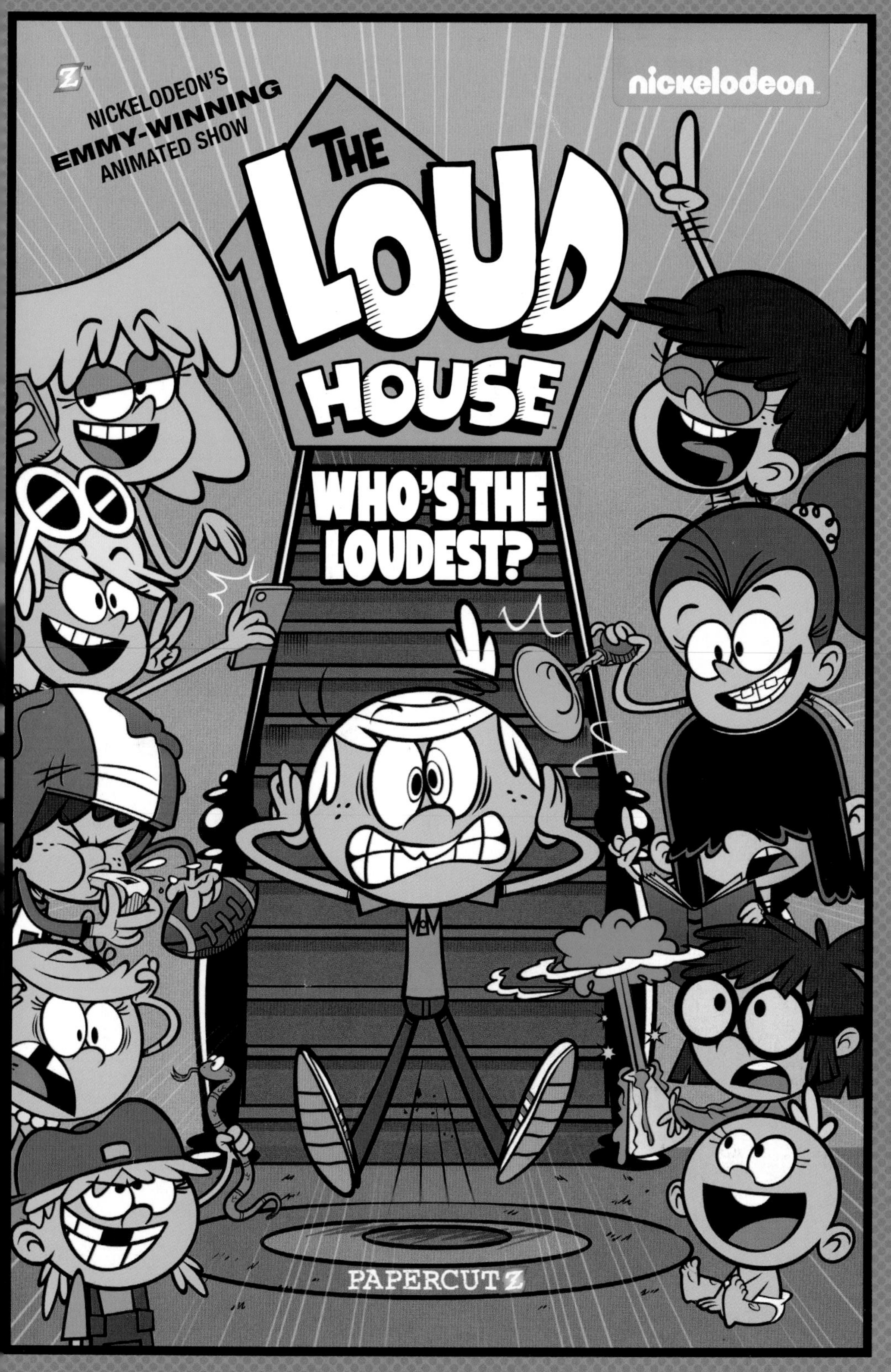

THE LOUD HOUSE #11 Cover Art by GABRIELLE DOLBEY and ZAZO AGUIAR

"I KNOW WHERE YOU SHOPPED LAST SUMMER"

THANKS FOR LETTING ME DRIVE VANZILLA, LENI. I REALLY WANT TO PRACTICE NOW THAT I HAVE MY LICENSE.
FUNG

OMGOSH! IT'S TOTALLY NO PROBLEM. ESPECIALLY SINCE WE'RE GOING TO--
NOM

THE NEW REININGER'S OUTLET STORE!
50% OFF
SALE
SALE

FUNG
LET'S SEE HOW THE HAZELTUCKY SALES TEAM HANDLES SEASONED BARGAIN HUNTERS LIKE US!

SCREECH
BA-BUMP

MY BABY BLUE POLISH!
MY FRIES!
"BA-BUMP?"

OH, NO, OH, NO! I TOTALLY DESTROYED YOUR FAMILY CAR. NOW YOUR PARENTS WILL NEVER LET US HANG OUT OUTSIDE OF WORK!

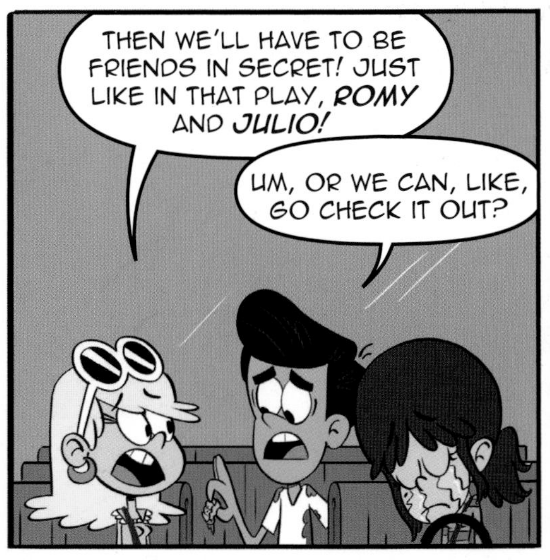
THEN WE'LL HAVE TO BE FRIENDS IN SECRET! JUST LIKE IN THAT PLAY, *ROMY* AND *JULIO!*
UM, OR WE CAN, LIKE, GO CHECK IT OUT?

SEE! IT'S JUST A FLAT TIRE.
WHAT A RELIEF!
YAY!

SO, UM... WHO KNOWS HOW TO FIX A FLAT TIRE?
DON'T LOOK AT ME! I *JUST* LEARNED HOW TO DRIVE!

*OMG*OSH! I HAVE THE *BEST* IDEA!

I'M GOING TO CHANNEL MY SISTER *LANA*. SHE'S THE BEST CAR-FIXER-PERSON I KNOW!
LENI, THAT'S REALLY SWEET BUT I DOUBT--

BURP! LET'S MAKE THIS PUPPY PURR!

POP

SQUEAK

OH, WOW! THIS IS ACTUALLY WORKING.
PLEASE, PLEASE, PLEASE!
FUNG

ALRIGHTY, GUYS. THAT SHOULD DO THE TRICK!

TO QUOTE ***LORI***, "YOU'RE ***LITERALLY*** THE BEST."
SALE
SALE

NOW, LET'S ROCK OUT 'TIL WE SHOP OUT!
LET'S GET SOME DRIVING TUNES ON!

SNAP

OR NOT...

OH!

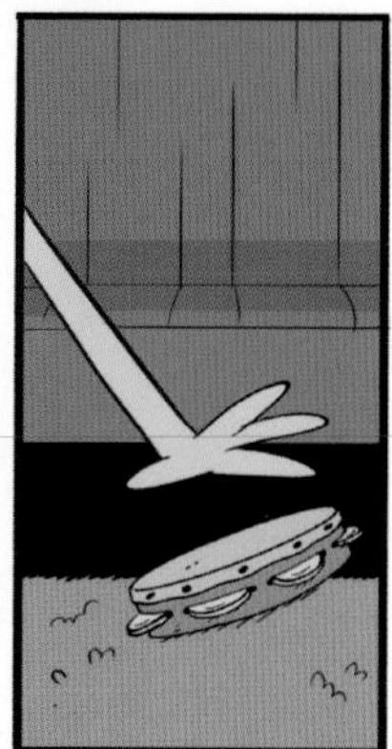

OR I CAN CHANNEL *LUNA* AND PLAY US OUT?

LA LA! OOH, GIRL!
OR MAYBE WE COULD, LIKE, TALK?
THAT TOTALLY WORKS!
POM POM POM
END

"HOME SICKNESS!"

Hectors_Scoop: ¡Tan hermosa! Both you and the tower!
Parrotlover123: Bring back a baguette for me!

Sk8_Dont_H8: Whoa, cool!! See any giant robots yet?
Bobby_BooBooBear: Please eat all the ramen for me.

BEST_ABUELA_EVER: How to peel tomatoes fast.
Fotografa_Frida Rosa, this isn't where you search the internet.

Captain_CJ: YARR, perfect place for a pirate!
Smoothtalker_Carl: Sure, if all a pirate wanted was to kick back all day.
BEST_ABUELA_EVER: How to peel potatoes fast

YOUR NEXT DESTINATION AWAITS, MIJA...

THANKS FOR MAKING MY SICK DAY MORE FUN, GUYS. ⁼SNIFF!⁼

END

"MUSICAL MYRTLE"

ENCORE! WHOO!

OOH! IS THAT THE NEW SCREECHERS RECORD, LUNA?

WHAT? HOW DO YOU KNOW ABOUT THEM, MYRTLE?
OH, WELL, YOU KNOW ME. JUST TRYING TO STAY "HIP" TO WHATEVER YOU KIDS ARE INTO.

THESE GUYS ARE TOTALLY RAD...

AWWW, WOULD YOU LOOK AT THAT?
...YOU'RE PROBABLY THINKING OF SOMEONE ELSE, MYRTLE-DUDE. THIS CAN'T BE YOUR SPEED.

� SIGH.⋰ IT'S ALL COMING BACK TO ME NOW.

LISTEN TO THIS!
CLICK

LUNA, DEAR, WANT TO HEAR HOW OLD MYRTLE MADE--
GUITAR SOLO!

LATER THAT NIGHT...
HELLO, ROYAL WOODS!

WHOOO, YEAH!
HEY, DOWN IN FRONT, DUDE!

SK

MYRTLE?!

WHOA, FAR OUT!
WHY DIDN'T YOU TELL ME MYRTLE WAS TOTALLY COOL?

MYRTLE! I NEVER KNEW YOU WERE SO ROCKINNN'!
HEHEHE, I TOLD YOU I'M ALWAYS "HIP" TO WHAT YOU KIDS ARE INTO!

YOU KIDDOS WANT TO GO BACKSTAGE?
HUH? YOU KNOW THE BAND?
KNOW THEM? HA! I KNIT THEIR WARDROBE ...

...FOR THEIR '"LOVESTRUCK"' ALBUM--THEY DEMANDED IT. I SEND THEM SCARVES AND SWEATERS EVERY WINTER!

WE WANNA GIVE A SPECIAL SHOUT OUT TO ONE OF OUR FAVORITE LADIES HERE WITH US TONIGHT!

THIS ONE GOES OUT TO THE ONE WHO HELPS US ROCK OUR SCARVES SO WELL... MYRTLE!
NO WAY!

HEY, MYRTLE, WHAT DO YOU SAY YOU KNIT ME A SWEATER LIKE THE "MOUTAIN FOLK" ALBUM?
BETTER, I CAN TEACH YOU HOW I MADE IT!

END

"OCEAN 11"

IN THE LOUD HOUSE, LIFE IS LIKE A BEACH.
BEACH!

AND SOMETIMES, IT REALLY IS THE BEACH!

GEE, I HOPE I DIDN'T FORGET ANYTHING.
I DON'T THINK.... THAT'S POSSIBLE. IT FEELS LIKE... YOU PACKED EVERYTHING.

JUST YANK IT OPEN WITH YOUR TEETH.
THAT WOULD BE HIGHLY NOT ADVISABLE. FIRST YOU MUST TWIST AND LOCK.
GNRR

KIDS, WHAT'S THAT OVER THERE SITTING ON THE ROCKS?

IT LOOKS LIKE THERE'S SOMETHING INSIDE. A MESSAGE IN A BOTTLE.

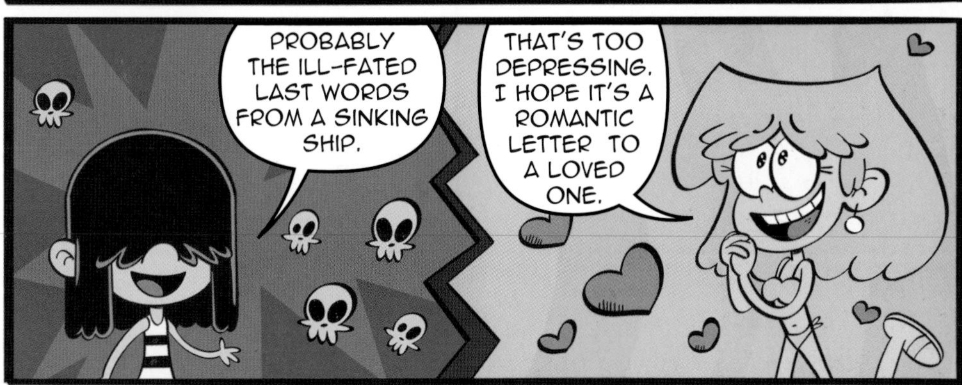
PROBABLY THE ILL-FATED LAST WORDS FROM A SINKING SHIP.
THAT'S TOO DEPRESSING. I HOPE IT'S A ROMANTIC LETTER TO A LOVED ONE.

LET'S BREAK IT OPEN AND SEE!
NO! IT'S TOO BEAUTIFUL TO DESTROY.
IF IT'S OLD, THE EXPOSURE TO AIR MIGHT DISSOLVE THE PAPER. THIS REQUIRES A MORE SCIENTIFIC SOLUTION.

ALLOW ME...
TAP
POP

ANY GOOD JOKES WRITTEN ON IT? I'LL EVEN TAKE BAD ONES.
NO, ***LUAN!*** IT'S A TREASURE MAP!

ACCORDING TO THIS MAP, IT LOOKS LIKE THERE ARE CLUES SCATTERED AROUND THE BEACH THAT WILL LEAD US TO THE BURIED TREASURE.
LET'S DO THIS!

I'M ALREADY ON IT!

I FOUND THE TREASURE!
EWWWW.... GROSS!

NO, THANKS. I'LL LOOK FOR LOST LOVE ELSEWHERE.

LET ME SEE THAT MAP!
HEY!
THE KIDS APPEAR TO BE HAVING FUN.

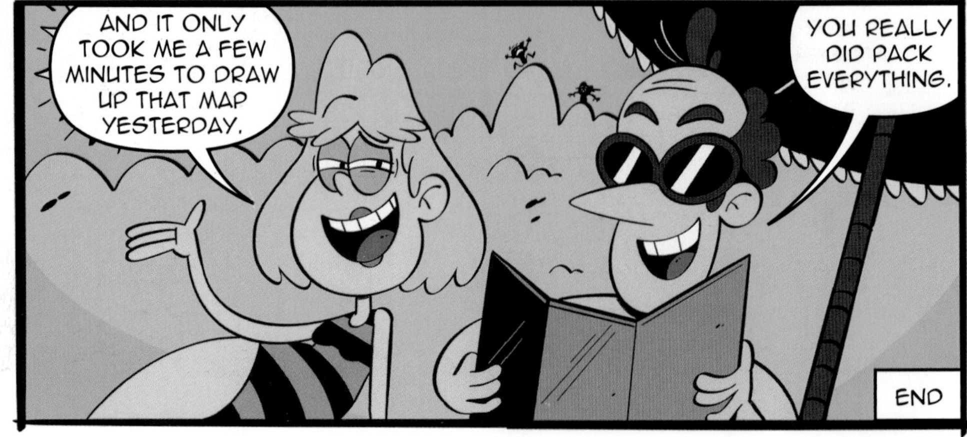
AND IT ONLY TOOK ME A FEW MINUTES TO DRAW UP THAT MAP YESTERDAY.
YOU REALLY DID PACK EVERYTHING.
END

"FREE TO BE ME"

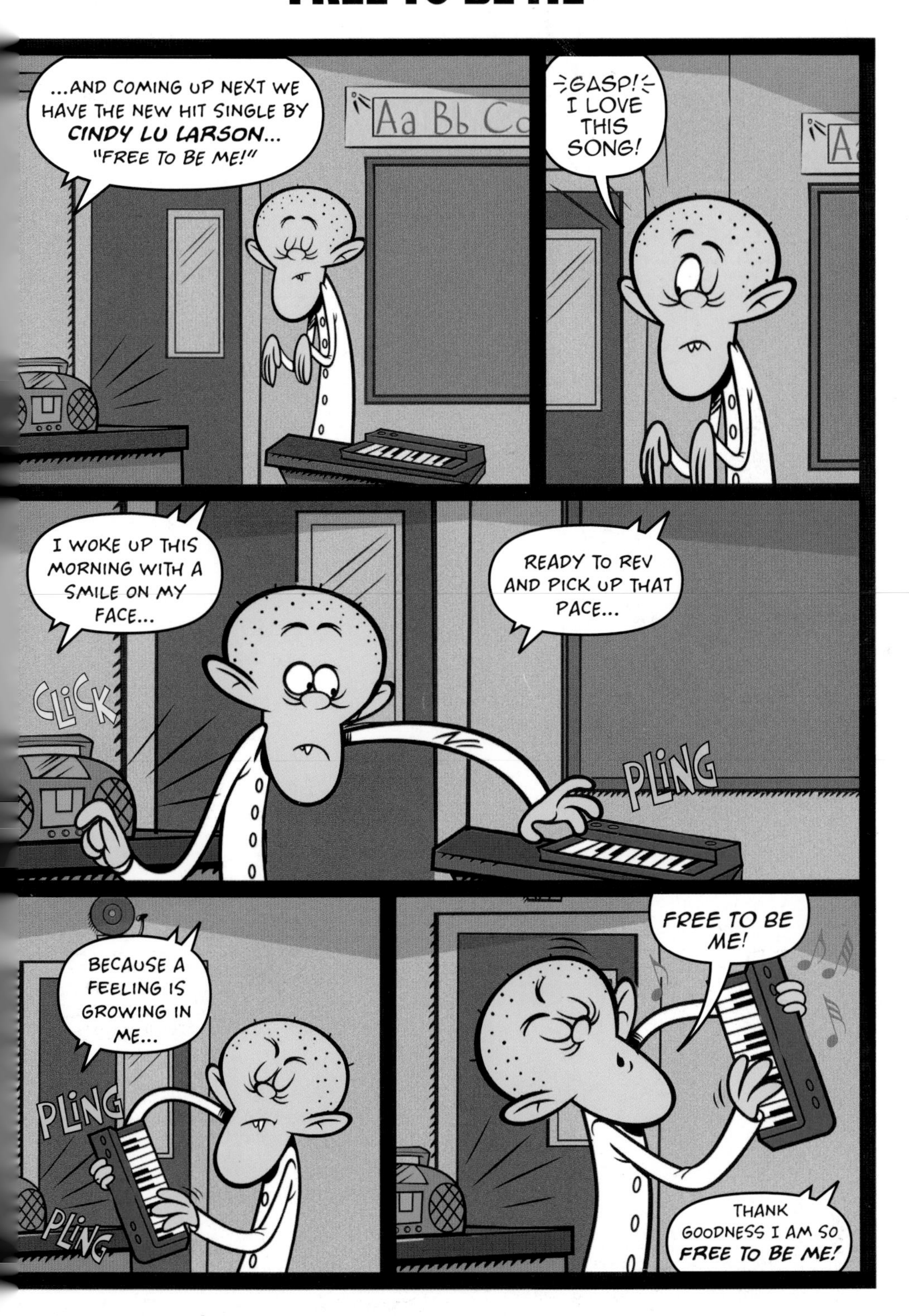

...AND COMING UP NEXT WE HAVE THE NEW HIT SINGLE BY CINDY LU LARSON... "FREE TO BE ME!"
Aa Bb Cc
GASP! I LOVE THIS SONG!
I WOKE UP THIS MORNING WITH A SMILE ON MY FACE...
CLICK
READY TO REV AND PICK UP THAT PACE...
PLING
BECAUSE A FEELING IS GROWING IN ME...
PLING
PLING
FREE TO BE ME!
THANK GOODNESS I AM SO FREE TO BE ME!

UH-HUH. SHAKE IT!
PLING
SING IT, CINDY LU!
PLING
PLING
I JUST HOPE THE MORTICIANS CLUB DON'T LEARN ABOUT--
...THIS.
BORIS...

THAT... WAS...
AMAZING!
Cc Dd Ee F
YOU DON'T CARE THAT BORIS LIKES A POP SONG?
OF COURSE NOT!
PLUS, IT SOUNDS GREAT ON FUNERAL ORGAN.
WHAT ARE YOU WAITING FOR, BORIS? KEEP ON PLAYING!
ALRIGHT, BERTRAND, TURN UP THE RADIO!
THANK GOODNESS I'M SO FREE TO BE ME!
Ff Gg Hh Ii
END

"SNACK ATTACK"

WOOF!
AH! LALO! WHAT'S GOTTEN INTO YOU?

WOOF!
SHH, LALO!

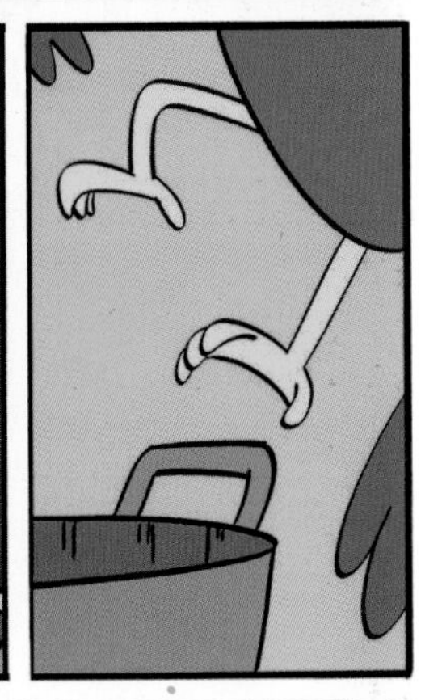

CLANG
IT ISN'T PLAYTIME RIGHT NOW.
RETREAT AND REGROUP! RETREAT AND REGROUP!
BOOF!

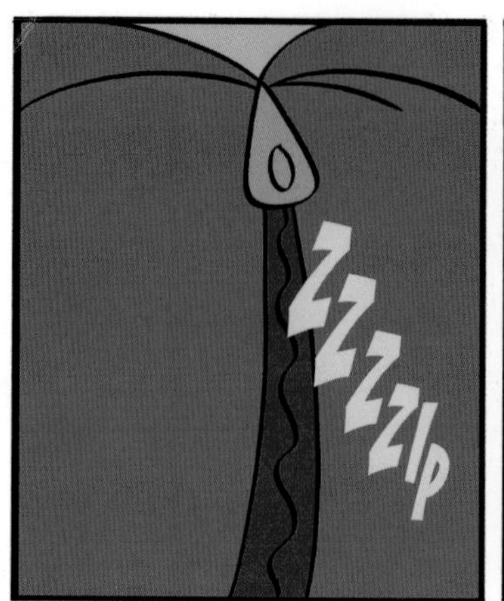
ZZZZZIP

BRAWK! LOOKIN' GOOD!

ARE YOU SICK, MIJA? YOU LOOK A LITTLE **FUNNY.**
I'M FINE!
YOU **SOUND** A LITTLE FUNNY TOO...

SERGIO?
ACK!
OUT WITH THE BOTH OF YOU!

LET ME COOK IN PEACE!

WHINE.
WE'RE FAILURES...
SERGIO! LALO!

I'VE BEEN WORKING ON THIS SPECIAL PET FOOD RECIPE ALL DAY, IF YOU WANT...

...SOME!
ZIP
ZIP

WELL, I GUESS YOU WERE HUNGRY!
CHOMP
CHOMP
MUNCH

WELL, THAT WAS EASY!
WOOF!
BURP
END

"THAT'S A WRAP"

END

"MACABRE MUNCHIES"

BLERG!

BANG BANG BANG

YOU WERE RIGHT, LUCY, THIS PLACE IS SCARY!
BORIS IS GOING TO BE SICK!
YEAH, IT SMELLS LIKE A MORGUE!
HEY, YOU KIDS!
FLiP's food & fuel
Special
toilet

COMPLAINTS COST A BUCK EACH! PAY UP AND TAKE THIS ICE QUEEN WITH YOU...
S-S-SO C-C-COLD...
COOL-ant
Choco Queen
SELF SERVE
SALE
$3.00 $2.49 a 2.00 QUART
OIL
the BOMB
GUM 49
Pickled eggs 25¢
15¢
No Refunds
THE END

"CANNONBALL RUN"

... SO THAT'S HOW I GOT THIS GIG...
ROYAL WOODS PUBLIC POOL

IT'S ONLY FOR A COUPLE SHIFTS BUT I'M READY TO MAKE SOME SUMMER CASH!
AWWW, BOO BOO BEAR. I'M SO HAPPY YOU'RE HERE, EVEN IF IT'S JUST FOR A FEW DAYS.

CANNONBALL!

SPLASH

GRRR, LYNN!

WHOOPS, SORRY, LORI. IT'S JUST THAT THE POOL IS SO EMPTY TODAY, I GUESS I GOT CARRIED AWAY.

CANNONBALL!

SPLASH

UGH.
HMM...

YOU KNOW, **LORI**, LYNN'S RIGHT. THE POOL'S USUALLY NOT THIS EMPTY, ESPECIALLY AT THIS TIME OF YEAR.

YEAH, **LISA**, TALK ABOUT BORING!
I CONCUR WITH THIS SENTIMENT.

WATER LAME WAY TO SPEND THE DAY.
YOU GUYS THINKING WHAT I'M THINKING...?
SWIMMING CONTEST!

ALRIGHT, LOUDS! FIRST TO MAKE IT TO THE FINISH LINE GETS BRAGGING RIGHTS FOR THE WHOLE SUMMER.

"ON THE COUNT OF THREE..

"1...

"2...

"3!
SLURP

"GO"
PLOP
PLOP
PLOP
PLOP
PLOP

ZOOM
SPLASH
WAS THAT LYNN?

AH... HI, BROTHER.
...HUH?
SLURP

GRUMBLE!

LYNN FOR THE WIN! LYNN FOR THE WIN!

AHHH, NOT COOL! CRAMP!

NOW'S MY CHANCE!
I BELIEVE THAT NOW IS AN OPPORTUNE TIME...

...TO TEST MY LATEST INVENTION.

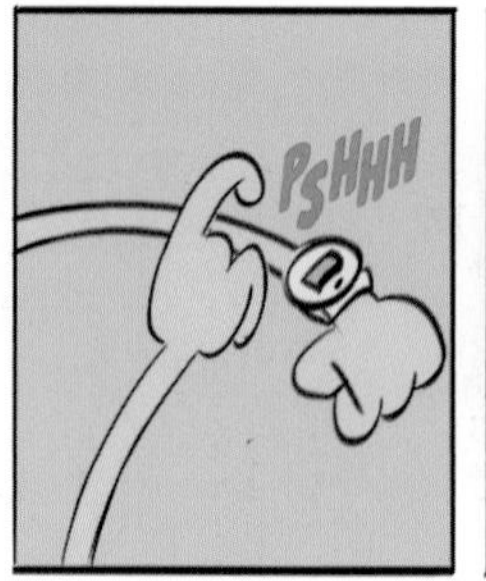
PSHHH

FWOOM

EUREKA! IT'S WORKING!

OH, DEAR.
BZZRT
PUTT
PUTT
PUTT

ALMOST THERE!

RUBBER DUCKY, YOU SAID ***YOU'RE THE ONE!*** ⇉HMPF!⇇

WOW, HE STILL HAS A SHOT.
LINCOLN MAY LITERALLY WIN!

ALMOST ⇉HUFF!⇇ ⇉PUFF!⇇ THERE!

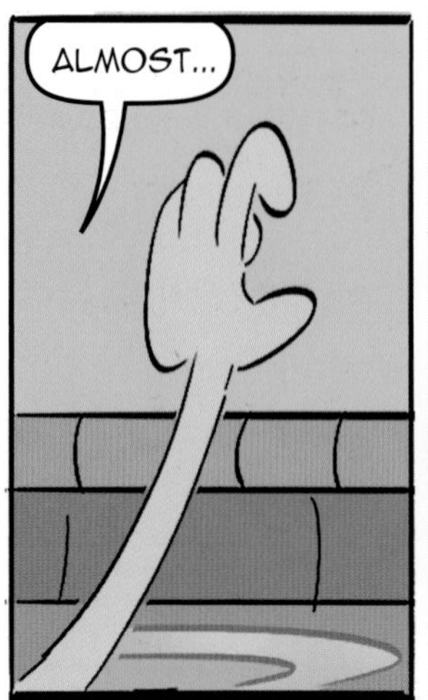
ALMOST...

HEAD FOR THE HILLS, SIBLINGS, POST HASTE!
SPITZ
SPUTTER

INSTEAD OF TREADING WATER, I AM RETAINING IT!
SLURP

I GOT NOTHING. THIS SUCKS THE FUN OUT OF IT, DOESN'T IT?
I DO FEEL A BIT MORE SHALLOW.
SLURP

I'M WINNING! IN YOUR **FACE,** LYNN!

DANG IT! WHERE'D THE WATER GO?
THUD

APOLOGIES, SIBLINGS, I SHOULD'VE MENTIONED THAT THESE WINGS HAVEN'T BEEN FIELD TESTED.
AWW, MAN, I WAS JUST ABOUT TO BEAT **STINKIN'.**

CAN SOMEBODY GET ME DOWN FROM HERE?

GRR! SOMEBODY SPILLED MY JUICE!
JUICED WHEN THIS DAY COULDN'T GET ANY WORSE, HUH, SIS?

MY POOL! MY JOB!

MY CONDOLENCES, BOBBY. BUT YOU'RE TALL, DO YOU MIND HELPING ME GET DOWN?

SIGH. GUESS IT'S TIME TO FIND A **NEW** SUMMER JOB...
THERE ARE LITERALLY PLENTY OF POOLS AROUND!

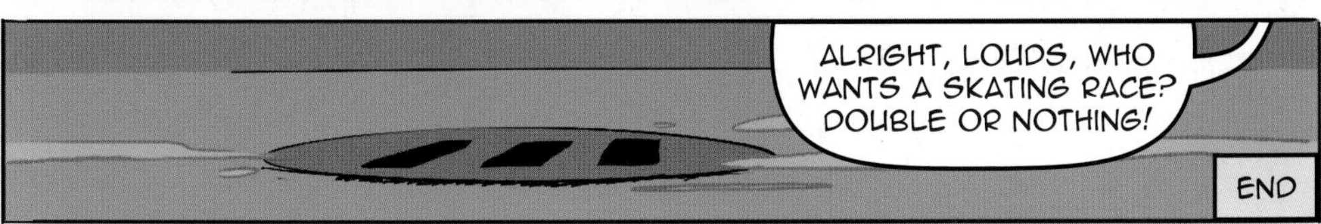
ALRIGHT, LOUDS, WHO WANTS A SKATING RACE? DOUBLE OR NOTHING!
END

"CUSTOMER APPRECIATION"

END

"ROBOT RUMPUS"

COME ON, LINC, GET UP!
SNORE
WE'LL BE RIGHT BACK TO ATTACK OF THE EVIL ROBOTS PART 15! AFTER A WORD FROM OUR SPONSERS... MIND CONTROL, IT'S CONTROL, FOR YOUR BRAIN!

LINCOLN!
AGH! ZACH?

SHH!
YOU'RE THE ONE WHO JUST SHOUTED ME AWAKE!
I KNOW, BUT THIS IS IMPORTANT. LOOK...

CLYDE'S BEEN REPLACED BY A ROBOT! JUST LIKE IN THE MOVIE!
HOW CAN YOU BE SURE?

JUST LOOK AT HIM... HIS MOVEMENTS ARE SO STIFF AND OVERLY COORDINATED!

YOU'RE RIGHT, THE REAL CLYDE TAKES WAY TOO MANY YOGA CLASSES TO MOVE SO STIFFLY.

DON'T WORRY, I'VE BEEN PREPARED FOR SOMETHING LIKE THIS. I HAVE GEAR, ARMOR...
WE HAVE NO CHOICE...

... I JUST NEED A LITTLE OF EVERY ROBOT'S BIGGEST WEAKNESS...
...WATER!

HE'S COMING!
READY... STEADY...

SPLASH
AUGH!

YEAH! WE TOTALLY SHORTED THE ROBOT OUT!
I TOLD YOU I WAS PREPA--

YOU GUYS!
WHAT GIVES?!

B-BUDDY? I THOUGHT YOU WERE A- A ROBOT!
WHAT, WHY?!
WELL, ZACH SAID THAT...

WHAT? NO! MY NEW DIETARY ROUTINE CAUSES SLEEPWALKING!
WHAT?

SLEEPWALKING, BODY SNATCHING ROBOTS, WHO CAN REALLY BE SURE THESE DAYS, HUH, GUYS? HEH. HEH.

HEY, BUDDY, IS ZACH A ROBOT?!
BETTER USE THESE WATER BALLOONS TO SHORT HIM OUT!
AHHH!
END

HOOK, LINE, AND STINKER

ALRIGHT, KIDDOS, GRAB YOUR GEAR AND LET'S GET FISHING!

OH, MAN! OH, MAN! MY POND SCUM SUPPLY WAS RUNNING SUPER LOW!

TODAY IS OUR ANNUAL FISHING TRIP WITH POP POP! I'M JUST HOPING I CATCH SOMETHING A LITTLE BIT BIGGER THAN LAST YEAR...

LAST YEAR...

DON'T WORRY, BUCK-O! WE'RE GONNA GET YOU A HECK-OF-A CATCH THIS YEAR.

IN FACT, I BROUGHT MY SECRET WEAPON!

YOUR POP POP'S SUPER SPECIAL, HOMEMADE
STINK BAIT!

NOW, LET'S GO CATCH OURSELVES SOME FISH!

LOLA! LORI! YOU GIRLS SURE YOU DON'T WANNA GRAB A REEL AND SNAG A BIG OL' FISH?

WE LOVE YOU, POP POP, BUT FISH ARE, LIKE, SUPER ICKY.

HAHA, ALRIGHT! SUIT YOURSELF! JUST MEANS MORE FOR US!

HEY, I THINK SOMETHING IS NIBBLING ON MY LIINE!
!

BLOOP

HOT DOG!
REEL IT IN!
REEL IT IN!
CRANK
CRANK
CRANK

DANG IT. THE FISH STOLE MY BAIT!
AH, IT'S OKAY, LINC! LET'S JUST SLAP SOME MORE OF THIS STINK BAIT ON THAT HOOK AND SEE IF WE CAN'T SNAG THAT FISH AGAIN!
THAT FISH WON'T GET AWAY NEXT TIME! MARK MY WORDS!
LATER...
HEY, POP POP! THAT FISH IS NIBBLING ON THE LINE AGAIN!
REEL IT IN! REEL IT IN!
PLOOP
DANG IT.

I'VE GOT AN IDEA!
WE'LL USE THE FISHING NET!
THE NEXT TIME YOU FEEL THAT FISH TRYING TO TAKE THE BAIT, I'LL SWOOP IN WITH THE NET!
SOON...
THE FISH IS BACK POP POP!
THERE'S NO GETTING AWAY FROM US NOW, FISH!
YOU GUYS GOT ANY MORE OF THAT TASTY STINK BAIT?
END

"ONE, TWO, SWITCHEROO"

ALRIGHT, THIS SHOULD SUFFICE...JUST A HINT OF BENZANOIDIC ALLOY...

A FEW HAIR FOLLICLE SAMPLES FROM MY TEST SUBJECTS... AND...

ALRIGHT, WHO'S READY TO TEST THIS **BRAIN SWITCHING** MACHINE OUT?

MEOW?

ZZZZAP

ANY RECOGNIZABLE CHANGES? MOLECULAR INSTABILITY? VARIATIONS IN BONE CHEMISTRY?
...

GRUMBLE. NOTHING. IT NEEDS SOME MINOR ADJUSTMENTS... IF ONLY I HAD... HMMM...

WOOF?!
MEOW?!

HISS!
GROWL!

CLACK

ZZZZAP

WAS THAT A BIO-MOLECULAR EXPLOSION I HEARD?

HRMM...

I'VE GOT TOO MUCH VIVACULAR MODIFICATION ON THE BRAIN TODAY...

CHIRP!?
SQUEAK!?
END?

"WHO'S THE LOUDEST?"

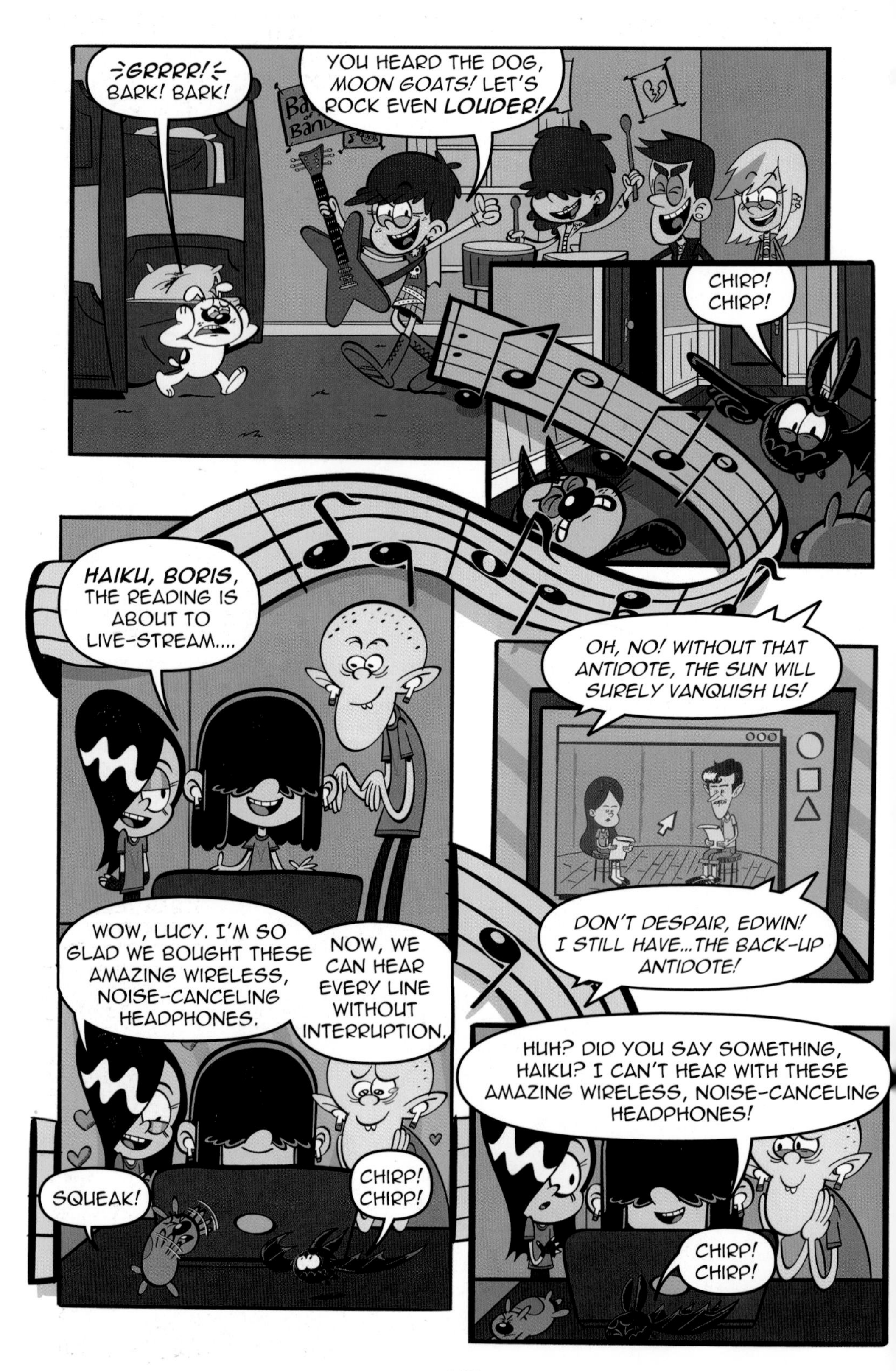
GRRRR! BARK! BARK!
YOU HEARD THE DOG, MOON GOATS! LET'S ROCK EVEN LOUDER!
CHIRP! CHIRP!
HAIKU, BORIS, THE READING IS ABOUT TO LIVE-STREAM....
OH, NO! WITHOUT THAT ANTIDOTE, THE SUN WILL SURELY VANQUISH US!
DON'T DESPAIR, EDWIN! I STILL HAVE...THE BACK-UP ANTIDOTE!
WOW, LUCY. I'M SO GLAD WE BOUGHT THESE AMAZING WIRELESS, NOISE-CANCELING HEADPHONES.
NOW, WE CAN HEAR EVERY LINE WITHOUT INTERRUPTION.
SQUEAK!
CHIRP! CHIRP!
HUH? DID YOU SAY SOMETHING, HAIKU? I CAN'T HEAR WITH THESE AMAZING WIRELESS, NOISE-CANCELING HEADPHONES!
CHIRP! CHIRP!

YAWN

THIS IS AS LOUD AS IT GETS... IT'S ON *FULL VOLUME, LILY.*

ANOTHER GOAL FOR THE JELLYFISH! COME ON, LILY, CHEER SO THAT THE PLAYERS CAN HEAR YOU!
GAH GOAL!

WIRR

EGAD! THAT'S NOT A BLENDER, IT'S MY NEW *NOISE-LOUDENING* DEVICE!
WIRRR
HUH? I CAN'T HEAR YOU OVER MY STRAWBERRY SMOOTHIE!

PHEW

YAWN!
SNORE! RIBBIT. RIBBIT. RIBBIT.
ZZ ZZZ ZZ ZZ

LET'S GET THIS CAST PARTY STARTED!
YAH! CAST PARTY!
I BROUGHT THE SHOW TUNES!
HA HA HA!

CONGRATS CAST OF 12 ANGRY MIMES!
RIGHT? I FEEL LIKE I HAVE SO MUCH PENT-UP NOISE TO MAKE!
THAT PLAY WAS FUN BUT I'M GLAD WE DON'T HAVE TO BE QUIET LIKE MIMES ANYMORE!
AH!

CAN YOU KIDS QUIET DOWN? I CAN'T HEAR MY MOWER MOW! AND THAT'S MY FAVORITE PART.
MRRRRR

QUIET! WE CAN'T HEAR THE GAME!
OMGOSH. I DIDN'T MAKE ENOUGH SMOOTHIES!
OUR HEADPHONES RAN OUT OF BATTERIES. SIGH.

MRR-MRR-MRR
BLAH BLAH BLAH!
I AM EXERCISING MY VOCAL CORDS!
LA LA LA LA LA LA LA...
HONK
CRUNCH
THINK OF THE STRAWBERRIES!
NO, BOO BOO BEAR, I CAN'T HEAR YOU! LET ME TRY SPEAKER PHONE.
THAT WAS THE GAME POINT!
GAME! GAME!
YOU EITHER RUINED OR IMPROVED MY INVENTION. WE NEED MORE NOISE!

CHEW
CHEW
HEY! WHERE'D THE ROCKIN' VOLUME GO?
AHH!
I'VE SEEN THIS MOVIE. CLASSIC.

OH, RIGHT. THEY WERE TRYING TO NAP.
WHY'D WE BUY THE CHIPS WITH THE EXTRA CRUNCH?!
CHIP

LUAN! IS IT TOO LATE TO PERFORM AT YOUR PARTY?
Z
Z

WOW. WHAT DID I SAY?
HONESTLY, IT'S FOR THE BEST.
HISS!
BARK!
RIBBIT!
TWEET!
END

NICKELODEON'S EMMY-WINNING ANIMATED SHOW

nickelodeon

THE LOUD HOUSE

THE CASE OF THE STOLEN DRAWERS

PAPERCUTZ

THE LOUD HOUSE #12 Cover Art by TODD OMAN

"THE CASE OF THE STOLEN DRAWERS"

"...AND I KNEW JUST THE CULPRITS TO TALK TO FIRST.
I TOLD YOU, LOUD! I DON'T KNOW ANYTHING!
WOOF!
"A DOG AND ITS MASTER, JUST AS THICK AS THIEVES...
SEE? NOW YOU'RE UPSETTING MY PRECIOUS FLUFFBALL.
I'M ACTUALLY JUST SAD ABOUT THE UNDERWEAR...
"IN MORE WAYS THAN ONE.
DOGS DON'T TALK, GENIUS!
OH, RIGHT... WOOF!
HEY, YOU TWO, FOCUS. THIS ISN'T A GAME.

"I'D ALREADY HAD ENOUGH OF THEIR SHENANI-GANS.
I NEED YOU TO COUGH UP THE INFORMATION, LOLA, OR WE'RE GONNA HAVE SOME PROBLEMS.
IT'S MISTER BEARDLY TO YOU! LOOK, WE KNOW NOTHING.
NOTHING.
"THEY WERE ALREADY CRACKING.
EHEHE... I MEAN, BARK BARK?
SO YOU DO KNOW SOMEONE, "FLUFF-BALL"? OR IS THAT EVEN YOUR REAL NAME?
QUIET, STINKY MUTT!
"I HAD THEM RIGHT WHERE I WANTED THEM. AND THE DOG WAS STINKY.
BUT WHERE WOULD A DOG PICK UP SO MUCH STENCH... OTHER THAN...

THE GARBAGE!
GOO!
"THERE IT WAS... A FAMILIAR SOUND, BUT SO FAR OFF... BUT I COULDN'T LET THE GHOSTS OF MY PAST DISTRACT ME. IT WAS TIME TO TAKE OUT THE TRASH.
"I WASN'T SURE IF I WAS GOING TO RUN INTO AN OLD FRIEND OR A RACCOON.
LYNN? ISN'T THIS MORE LANA'S THING?
RUSTLE RUSTLE RUSTLE
"IT TURNED OUT TO BE A BIT OF BOTH.
WHO YOU CALLIN' LAN--UH... OH! HEY, PAL, LONG TIME NO SEE! WANT A BITE? IT'S ONLY FROM YESTERDAY!
UH, NO THANKS. I'VE GOT INDIGESTION.
"THE KIND OF INDIGESTION YOU GET AROUND A CRIMINAL.
SUIT YOURSELF. ME, I'M ROLLING IN IT. STINKING FILTHY RICH. MINUS THE RICH...
DID YOU HAPPEN TO FIND ANY UNDERWEAR, AT LEAST?
NAH, BUT YOU KNOW, I HEARD THE FOOTBALL COACH WAS LOOKING FOR SOME LUCKY UNDIES FOR THE TEAM...
"SOMETIMES, THOUGH, HELP COMES FROM THE DIRTIEST PLACES. OR, AT LEAST, I HAD HOPED.
THANK YOU! ENJOY THAT HOT DOG FOR ME!
OH, BUDDY, WAY AHEAD OF YA.

"BUT TIME WAS RUNNING OUT, AND LEADS KEPT GOING NOWHERE...
LUNA? YOU'RE THE COACH?
WHO'S THIS "LUNA" YOU'RE TALKING ABOUT, SON?
"IDENTITIES BECAME MORE AND MORE CONFUSED, AND THE TRAIL BECAME ALMOST TOO FAINT TO SEE...
THE NAME'S COACH. COACH ROCKOWSKI. BESIDES, THERE'S NO WAY I'D STEAL ONE PAIR OF UNDERWEAR FOR AN ENTIRE TEAM!
MY PLAYERS ARE EXPECTED TO BRING THEIR LUCKY GARMENTS FROM HOME!
"IN FACT, THE FARTHER DOWN THE RABBIT HOLE I DOVE...
I'M SORRY, BUT EW? HYGIENE IS VERY IMPORTANT TO US FOOTBALL PLAYERS.
YEAH, MAYBE I SHOULDN'T HAVE ASKED YOU...
"THE FARTHER I FELL FROM MY PRECIOUS LUCKY UNDERWEAR.
WHAT COULD I POSSIBLY WANT WITH YOUR UNDER-WEAR? I'M JUST THE GARDENER.
"UNTIL IT SEEMED LIKE A DOOMED MISSION ENTIRELY.
SIGH. CAN I JUST LEAVE?
YEAH, YOU'RE GOOD TO GO.
HAVE A HAPPY DAY.
I WAS SO SURE I WOULD BE ABLE TO SOLVE THIS CAPER...

"BUT IT SEEMED LIKE I TRULY WOULD NEVER SEE MY LUCKY UNDERWEAR AGAI--
BUTT!
"BUT WAIT, THERE IT WAS AGAIN... THE CALL OF A BABY, JUST BEYOND MY REACH!
LILY?
BUTT!
LILY! WHERE ARE YOU?!
"HAD MY QUEST TO FIND MY LUCKY DRAWERS DRIVEN ME TO MADNESS?
"WOULD I EVER RECOVER? WOULD MY UNDERWEAR EVER BE FOUND? A MILLION QUESTIONS FILL MY HEAD...
BUTT! BUTT!
BUTT!
GOO! BUTT!
LILY... LILY...
BUTT!
BUTT!
"AND THOSE QUESTIONS SPAN UNTIL I WAS...
LILY, I CAN'T FIND YOU! LILY--
BUTT!
BUTT!
BUTT!
BUTT!
AUGH!

LILY? I JUST HAD THE WEIRDEST DREAM... I THOUGHT I LOST MY--

--MY LUCKY UNDERWEAR!

COME ON, COME ON, WHERE ARE THEY?
BUTT!

OH...WHAT? I COMPLETELY FORGOT, I MUST HAVE GONE TO SLEEP IN THESE AND FORGOTTEN... THANKS, LILY.

BUT WAIT...
LILY, YOU'RE MISSING YOUR DIAPER! YOU KNOW WHAT THAT MEANS...
"IT WAS TIME FOR ANOTHER INVESTIGATION. AFTER ALL... A GOOD DETECTIVE NEVER RESTS. ESPECIALLY NOT WHEN HE'S WEARING HIS LUCKY DRAWERS."
THE END

"GOING COCO-NUTS!"

BOY, BLASTING ALIENS SURE DOES WORK UP A SWEAT.
PING
NOTHING LIKE SOME GOOD OL' LEMONADE TO GIVE ME A MUCH NEEDED BOOST.
HUH? MR. COCONUTS?
WEIRD. I'LL GO ASK LUAN...
HEY, DO YOU MIND TAKING MR. COCONUTS OFF THE COUCH? I WAS IN THE MIDDLE OF SOMETHING AND HE'S ON THE REMOTE. ALSO, IS HE... ANGRY?
I WISH I COULD BUT HE'S GIVING ME THE SILENT TREATMENT.

WE HAD A ROUGH SET AT THE OLD FOLKS HOME RECENTLY AND HE DIDN'T TAKE IT TOO WELL.
UH-HUH.
YOU SHOULD TRY TALKING TO HIM, SEE IF HE'S STILL UPSET.
HEY, MR. COCONUTS. HOW ARE YOU FEELING AFTER YESTERDAY?
EVERYTHING'S JUST SWELL WITH ME, TOOTS.
OH, WELL THAT'S GOO--
I WAS *JOKING!* *AM I OKAY? AM I OKAY?* YOU LET ME FLOP LIKE A PIECE OF DRIFTWOOD OUT THERE!

DON'T TAKE THAT TONE WITH ME, MR. C!
LET'S FACE IT, DOLL, I'M THE ONE WHO'S BEEN PROPPING YOU UP ALL ALONG. I THINK IT'S TIME MR. C WENT SOLO!
THAT'S IT!
GUYS! LOOK...SOMETIMES YOU'LL HAVE BAD SHOWS BUT EVERY COMIC DUO NEEDS A PARTNER. NOW COME ON, SHAKE HANDS AND MAKE UP.
TELL MR. C, FINE BUT I DON'T WANNA SHAKE HANDS...
MR. COCONUTS, SHE'S FINE BUT SHE DOESN'T WANT TO SHAKE YOUR HAND.
DITTO,KID. TELL LUAN THAT I'LL CONSIDER TOUGHING THIS OUT WITH HER.
SIGH. DID YOU CATCH, THAT LUAN?
HERE. WHY DON'T YOU BOTH JUST WATCH SOME TV AND UNWIND?
HMPH.

I'LL BE UPSTAIRS.
SLAM
AND...SCENE! LUAN, DOLL! YOU WERE THE BEE'S KNEES. NOW THAT TV IS OURS!
AWW, THANKS, MR. C, YOU GAVE A PRETTY "POLISHED" PERFORMANCE YOURSELF!
LOOKS LIKE WE'RE JUST IN TIME FOR THE NEW "LAFF-FEST"!
SWOOP
PASS THE POPCORN, WILL YA?
END

"OLLIE OLLIE OXEN FREE"

I'VE BEEN WANTING TO LEARN HOW TO SKATE SO I COULD SURPRISE RONNIE ANNE WITH SOME COOL MOVES BUT...
...I WAITED TOO LONG AND NOW IT'S RAINING AND THERE'S NOWHERE TO PRACTICE.
"THERE'S NO SPACE IN THE HALLWAY DURING A RAINY DAY... THAT'S FOR SURE!
"LUCY'S WATCHING 'VAMPIRES OF MELANCHOLIA' IN THE LIVING ROOM, ACCORDING TO HER, IT'S THE PERFECT ATMOSPHERE.
"LANA HAS DIBS ON THE TREEHOUSE DURING RAINY DAYS SINCE THAT'S WHERE SHE SHELTERS HER WORMS."
WORST OF ALL, LYNN IS AT BASKETBALL CAMP... SO SHE'S NOT HERE SO I KINDA NEED YOUR GUYS' HELP. SID TOLD ME YOU'RE REALLY GOOD SKATERS.
SURE, WE'LL HELP YOU OUT!
AWESOME IDEA.
GO WE
DUDE, WE GOT YOU COVERED!

YOU NEED TO LEARN ABOUT BALANCE...
YEAH, BUT WHAT'S A GOOD TRICK TO START OFF WITH IN YOUR TINY ROOM.
IN KANSAS THERE WEREN'T MANY RAMPS OR RAILS SO I'D PRACTICE OLLIES!
GO WE
OKAY, I'VE HEARD OF OLLIES, SAMEER. HERE GOES NOTHING!
CRASH
THAT LOOKED LIKE IT REALLY HURT.
NIKKI, THAT ONE HURT ME...
GO WE
OOF!
YOU COULD REALLY USE SOME PADS.
GOOD IDEA, CASEY. I KNOW WHERE I COULD GET SOME.
YOU'RE GONNA FALL ON YOUR ELBOWS... A LOT.
CRRRP

DON'T FORGET TO PROTECT YOUR BUTT!
LAST BUT NOT LEAST, MAKE SURE YOU'RE WEARING A HELMET!
COINS
OKAY! NOW I'M READY TO ROLL.
WHOA! TALK ABOUT D.I.Y.!
SWEET!
NOW TRY THAT OLLIE AGAI--
CLANG
HEY, GUYS, READY TO GO?
WHOOPS!
FORGOT WE WERE MEETING UP WITH RONNIE ANNE TODAY.
LATER, LINCOLN!
BZZZT
BEEP
Sorry! RA is here. Call her uncle Carlos, he's the "X"-pert...
CALL THE "X"-PERT...?

THAT'S QUITE A PREDICAMENT YOU'RE IN, LINCOLN!
SINCE YOU'RE INDOORS, WE COULD PRACTICE A SIMPLE *POP MUSKRAT-FLIP.*
SOUNDS SIMPLE ENOUGH. THANKS, *CARLOS!*
AMAZING SPACE
THE MOST IMPORTANT PRINCIPLE IS BALANCE. KICK THE BOARD UP WITH YOUR RIGHT FOOT AND GENTLY SLIDE YOUR LEFT FOOT TO THE SIDE.
GOT IT!
CRASH
REMEMBER, LINCOLN, BALANCE!
OW! WAIT, ALMOST GOT IT, OW!
BANG
OH, DEAR.

HAH!
LANDED IT!
COINS
EXCELLENT JOB, LINCOLN!
YEAH... THANKS FOR THE HELP BUT I NEED TO CLEAN THIS UP...
YOUR ROOM, HOWEVER, HAS SEEN BETTER DAYS.
KIIIIDS! HAS ANYONE SEEN MY PASTA STRAINER? I'M MAKING MY RAINY DAY SPAGHETTI!
GULP!
END

"TONGUE-TIED"

IS THIS TURKEY OR HAM? I'LL ASK ROSA AND HECTOR.
Jamon

IS THIS TURKEY OR HAM?
IT'S IMPOSSSIBLE! THEY CAN'T SEE ALL OF GREAT LAKE CITY IN JUST ONE DAY...
HOLA, VITO. SORRY, WE ARE SUPER OCUPADOS...
Jamon

WE HAVE VISITORS COMING TOMORROW AND WE NEED TO SHOW THEM AROUND.

I CAN SHOW THEM MY FAVORITE ITALIAN RESTAURANT...?
THAT'S VERY NICE OF YOU, BUT OUR GUESTS ONLY SPEAK SPANISH.

HEY, VITO, ARE YOU GOING TO BUY THE JAMÓN?
THE WHAT?
Jamon

I REALLY NEED TO LEARN TO SPEAK SPANISH. HOW HARD CAN IT BE?
THEN I COULD HELP ROSA AND HECTOR... AND KNOW WHAT JAMÓN IS!

I BET I CAN FIND SOMETHING ONLINE THAT'LL SOLVE EVERYTHING!
I'LL BE FLUENT IN SPANISH BY TOMORROW. THEY'LL SEE!

THIS IS JUST WHAT I NEED...
SPANISH TO ENGLISH TRANSLATOR
-PERFECT FOR BEGINNERS- NOW WITH AUDIO NARRATION FOR EASY CONVERSATIO
BUY

IT'S ALL INSTALLED! I'LL JUST PRESS *TRANSLATE* AND SEE WHAT HAPPENS...
BIP

¿VIO MI PERRO?
DID YOU SEE MY DOG?

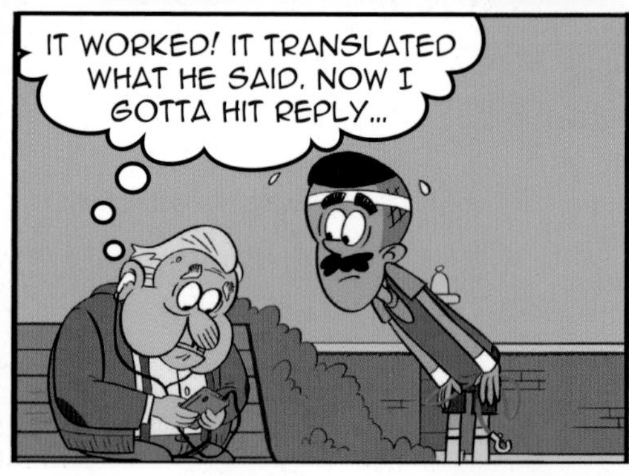
IT WORKED! IT TRANSLATED WHAT HE SAID. NOW I GOTTA HIT REPLY...

POSSIBLE RESPONSES
SORRY, I DON'T KNOW.
HE WENT THAT WAY.
TURN LEFT.
TURN RIGHT.
HE'S BEHIND YOU.
I'LL PRESS THIS ONE...

VAYA A LA DERECHA.
¡GRACIAS!
THANK YOU!

¿SEÑOR, LE GUSTARÍA UN HELADO?
DO YOU WANT ICE CREAM, SIR?

¡SÍ, POR FAVOR!

I AM GETTING THE HANG OF THIS WHOLE SPANISH THING.
SLURP

¿DONDE ESTA EL MERCADO?
WHERE IS THE MARKET?
I JUST CHOOSE "TURN LEFT THEN RIGHT."
GIRE A LA IZQUIERDA Y LUEGO A LA DERECHA.
GIRE A LA IZQUIERDA Y LUEGO A LA DERECHA.

WOW, VITO, I SAW WHAT JUST HAPPENED! YOUR SPANISH **HAS** IMPROVED.
MAYBE YOU CAN HELP ME WITH THE TOUR AFTER ALL. I'LL MEET YOU HERE IN THE MORNING!

¡SÍ, GRACIAS!

THE NEXT MORNING...
CHIPS! $1.99
HUH? WHY ISN'T THIS DARN PHONE TURNING ON? OH, NO! THE BATTERY IS DEAD... AND SO AM I!

HOLA, VITO, READY TO GIVE THE TOUR? THESE ARE OUR *VISITAS*. THE HERNANDEZ FAMILY.

UH... *¿SÍ?*
GO AHEAD DO YOUR THING.

CHIPS! $1.99
BUEN BURRITOS! WELCOME.

DO YOU MEAN "*BIENVENIDOS*"?
OH, YEAH, THAT'S WHAT I MEANT.

DID SOMEONE SAY GOOD BURRITOS? YOU'VE COME TO THE RIGHT SPOT! ¿ALGUIEN QUIERE UN BURRITO PARA LLEVAR?*
*TRANSLATION: ANYONE WANT A BURRITO TO GO?

VITO, DEAR, NOT HUNGRY? YOU LOOK PALE. ¿QUÉ PASA?
UH, WELL--

OUCH! ¡ME HUELE!
BONK

¡JA
JA
JA
JA!

WHAT DID I SAY?
YOU SAID "I SMELL." "HUELE" MEANS SMELL. "DUELE" MEANS HURT. COMMON MISTAKE.

SORRY, HECTOR, ROSA. I'M AN IMPOSTOR!

ONE WEEK LATER...
HI, VITO. IT IS GOOD TO SEE YOU AGAIN, WE HAVEN'T SEEN YOU AROUND.
I'M SORRY ABOUT THE OTHER DAY. I JUST GOT CARRIED AWAY.

I THOUGHT I FOUND A SHORT CUT, BUT I SHOULD LEARN BY LISTENING, NOT USING A DOOHICKEY.

I GUESS I'LL NEVER LEARN SPANISH...
YOU'RE BEING TOO HARD ON YOURSELF. LEARNING A LANGUAGE TAKES TIME.

I'LL TAKE THIS *JAMÓN*, PLEASE.
VITO! THAT'S ***SPANISH!*** SEE? YOU'RE LEARNING!
CHIPS!
Jamon

HOW ABOUT I TEACH YOU SOME SPANISH AND YOU TEACH ME SOME ITALIAN?
THERE'S ONE WORD I'VE ALWAYS KNOWN.

WHAT'S THAT?
AMIGO.
CLINK
THE END

"ZACH AND THE MEAN CHALK"

DETENTION IS POINTLESS, WHEN THERE'S A MONSTER AROUND.
IS ANYONE LISTENING?!
PRINCIPAL HUGGINS

SWOOSH

"LOOKING FOR ANSWERS? MEET ON THE PLAYGROUND NEAR THE MONKEY BARS."
Looking for answers? Meet on the playground near the monkey bars.

GURDLE? WHERE DID HE GO?

THIS IS THE SPOT WHERE THE NOTE SAID TO MEET.

WHOEVER YOU ARE...TAKE ME TO YOUR LEADER.
ACTUALLY, I THINK YOU'RE MISTAKEN.

WE'RE MORE OF A PARTNERSHIP.
CLINCOLN McCLOUD IS READY TO TAKE YOUR CASE.
WE'RE IN DANGER. THERE'S A CHALK MONSTER AT THIS SCHOOL. I CAN FEEL IT!
HMM. THAT SOUNDS HARD TO BELIEVE. BUT WORTH FINDING OUT.
GOT ANY PROOF?
THESE CHALK TRAILS ARE EVERYWHERE.
AND ITS CHALKY BREATH LINGERS IN THE AIR.
IT LEAVES ITS MARK ON WHATEVER IT TOUCHES.
A GOOD START. BUT THIS REQUIRES FURTHER INVESTIGATION.
MIGHT I SUGGEST, FINDING WITNESSES TO INTERROGATE?

FESS UP, ARTIE! HAVE YOU SEEN THE CHALK MONSTER?
WHAT THE HECK KIND OF QUESTION IS THAT? THAT SOUNDS STUPID.

IT'S A MONSTER MADE OUT OF CHALK, JOY.
EWWWW! I HOPE THAT'S NOT TRUE. I HATE GETTING CHALK DUST IN MY HAIR.

IT'LL NEVER CATCH THE RUST MAN. I'M TOO FAST!
THEN WHY'S YOUR BIKE STILL LOCKED UP?
I LOST THE COMBINATION.

I DIDN'T DO IT. I SWEAR!
DO WHAT?
IS THIS A POP QUIZ?

SKREEETCH
QUIET, PAPA WHEELIE!
DID YOU HEAR THAT?

THE SOUND CAME FROM OUT HERE.
JANITOR

COFF
COFF
WHEEEEEZE
SKUFF SKUFFLE

SHAKE-A-SHAKE-A-SHAKE
GAAAAAAHHHHH!

WHEW! IT'S ONLY JANITOR NORM.
DID HE FIGHT THE MONSTER?

YOU MIGHT SAY THAT.
THOSE CHALKBOARDS DON'T CLEAN THEMSELVES, Y'KNOW.

ANOTHER CASE SOLVED BY THE TEAM OF...
...CLINCOLN MCCLOUD!

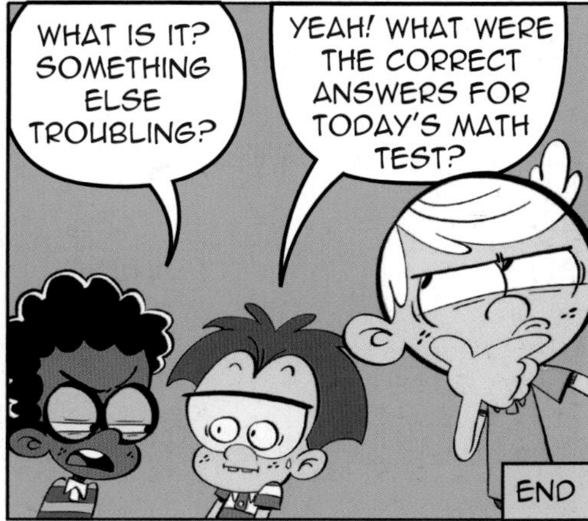
WHAT IS IT? SOMETHING ELSE TROUBLING?
YEAH! WHAT WERE THE CORRECT ANSWERS FOR TODAY'S MATH TEST?
END

"COMIC RELIEF"

MUAHAHAHAHA!
IS IT JUST ME, OR DO YOU HEAR THE SOUND OF DIABOLICAL LAUGHTER?
I THINK THAT'S JUST MY STOMACH. I DIDN'T EAT BREAKFAST.
GRUMBLE
RONNIE ANNE? I DIDN'T KNOW YOU WERE COMING TO THE COMIC SWAP!
SORRY, I DIDN'T TEXT YOU.
SERGIO FELT KINDA BASHFUL ABOUT DEBUTING HIS ORIGINAL COMIC SERIES...
LAS AVENTURAS DEL SERGIO EL MAGNÍFICO.
YOU SAID I WOULDN'T KNOW ANYBODY HERE!
COME ON, SERGIO. YOU'LL NEVER GET PAST THE RETIREMENT COMMUNITY CIRCUIT IF YOU DON'T PROUDLY DISPLAY YOUR WORK!
GRUMBLE
AY! YOU TWO MUST BE HUNGRY!
RONNIE ANNE, WHERE DID I PUT THOSE TAMALES?
STOP THAT MAID!
YOU KNOW I CAN'T RUN BEFORE YOGA!
HA HA! SORRY, JOKERS, BUT THE COMIC'S MINE NOW!
ACE SAVVY
JUSTICE IN SPADES
THIS LOOKS LIKE A JOB FOR...

ACE SAVVY AND ONE-EYED JACK!
WERE THOSE COSTUMES UNDER YOUR CLOTHES THE WHOLE TIME?
ALWAYS!
MUAHAHAHAHA!
HERE! PUDDIN'!
PLOP PLOP
OH, NO! SHE'S GOT PUDDING!
WHAT A DELICIOUS AND SLIPPERY OBSTACLE!
SLIP
I GOT YOU, ACE!
RONNIE ANNE! YOU STOP SKATEBOARDING INDOORS AT ONCE!
SORRY, ABUELA.
SCREECH
LOOKS LIKE YOU NEED SOME INDOOR WHEELS!

OH, NO! OUTTA GAS!
VROO-KA-POOT
PERFECT! NOW IT'S TIME TO UNSWAP!
AAH, I'M PANICKING UNDER PRESSURE!
BAP
FWIP FWIP
GASP!
HMMM, THIS LOOKS LIKE A JOB FOR SERGIO EL MAGNÍFICO.
SIGH. FINE, BUT I GET AN EXTRA TAMALE!

WOOSH
GOT!
YAY! YOU REALLY ARE MAGNIFICO!
YOU DID IT!
THAT WAS... PRETTY SUPER.
BOP
DANG IT, NOW HOW AM I GOING TO ENJOY THE COMIC SWAP?
HMMM...I THINK I HAVE AN IDEA.
SO, HOW ABOUT OUR NEXT CROSSOVER? TALK TO MY AGENT.
CAREFUL, BIRD, YOU'RE GETTING THE PAGES WET!
PASS THE BUTTER, MUSCLES.
SERGIO'S ABOUT TO GET A NEW ARCH NEMESIS!
THE END

"LEVEL UP"

LALO! SERGIO! IT'S TIME TO EAT!
CLANG CLANG
MÍ CASA es SU CASA

THERE YOU GO, LALO. WHERE'S YOUR FEATHERED FRIEND?
ARF?

HOLA, ABUELA.
RONNIE ANNE! HAVE YOU SEEN SERGIO ANYWHERE?

HMM... IS HE WITH BOBBY?
I DON'T THINK SO... I'M NOT SURE WHERE HE COULD BE--
PLAYER ONE WINS!
BRAWK!! THAT'S HOW IT'S DONE!

GET READY FOR ROUND TWO, SUCKERS!
HEY! I DIDN'T SAY YOU COULD USE MY LAPTOP!

I'M PLAYING CAVECRAFT!
WELL, STOP PLAYING, IT'S TIME TO EAT!

NO! I JUST LEVELED UP MY DARK MAGE!
YEAH, ON MY COMPUTER!

HEY, DON'T IGNORE ME!
CAN'T HEAR YOU, BRAWK! I'M BUSY.

RRGH, I NEED THAT COMPUTER FOR HOMEWORK! WE NEED TO GET IT AWAY FROM HIM!
BUT HOW? HE'S A VERY STUBBORN PARROT.

I THINK I HAVE AN IDEA...

BUT WE'RE GOING TO NEED SOME HELP.

ARRRGH! TASTE MY SWORD!

OH, NO, IT'S THE SWORD OF BLACKBEARD! THAT'S A PLUS TEN TO YOUR ATTACK POINTS!
ATTACK POINTS...?

BUT LITTLE DID YOU KNOW, I BROUGHT A STRENGTH POTION!
PSH, YOU THINK THAT'S GOING TO TURN THIS FIGHT IN YOUR FAVOR?
HEY...

WHAT ARE YOU GUYS PLAYING?
OH, JUST THE MOST FUN GAME EVER. BUT YOU'RE PROBABLY TOO BUSY WITH YOUR COMPUTER GAME TO PLAY, ANYWAYS...

GET READY TO LOSE, COUSIN!
IN YOUR DREAMS!

EN GARDE!

RONNIE ANNE! CJ! CARL! IT'S TIME FOR DINNER!
ALL RIGHT!
FOOD? TIME TO REPLENISH MY HEALTH POINTS!
GLUG GLUG

STILL WANT TO STAY ON THE COMPUTER?
...

ALRIGHT, SUIT YOURSELF...

SO? DID YOU GET SERGIO OFF OF THE COMPUTER?
NAH... BUT WE HAD FUN ANYWAY... I JUST HOPE I CAN GET MY COMPUTER BACK IN TIME TO--
WAIT!

BRAWK! DON'T FORGET ABOUT ME!

I THINK I'M READY TO LEVEL UP.
THE END

"MEAT YOUR MAKER"

THEY CAN'T MAKE ME EAT THIS!
⁼SIGH.⁼
GO NUTS!

I DON'T KNOW. MAYBE IT ACTUALLY TASTES GOOD?
EWWWWWW

IT'S NOT JUST THE TASTE WE SHOULD BE WORRIED ABOUT...
THE TEXTURE IS SUPER STRANGE!
SHCLUCK

IT DON'T LOOK LIKE NUTHIN' MY MEE-MAW MAKES BACK ON THE FARM.
GNAWWW
MILK 90%

THAT'S BECAUSE IT'S NOT FROM ANY ANIMAL ON THIS EARTH... IT'S FROM AN ALIEN!

IT'S ALL A COVER-UP. A SCHOOL GRAVY COVER-UP, I TELL YA!

IT'S UP TO US TO GET TO THE BOTTOM OF IT. AND FIND OUT WHAT THIS MYSTERY MEAT REALLY IS.

EXIT

FROZEN
CAFE

FOO

MEAT

♪
MEAT
MEAT

AHEM!

WE'VE TRIED EVERYTHING. BUT WE CAN'T TAKE IT ANYMORE. WE ONLY WANT THE TRUTH--
WHAT'S IN THE MYSTERY MEAT?!

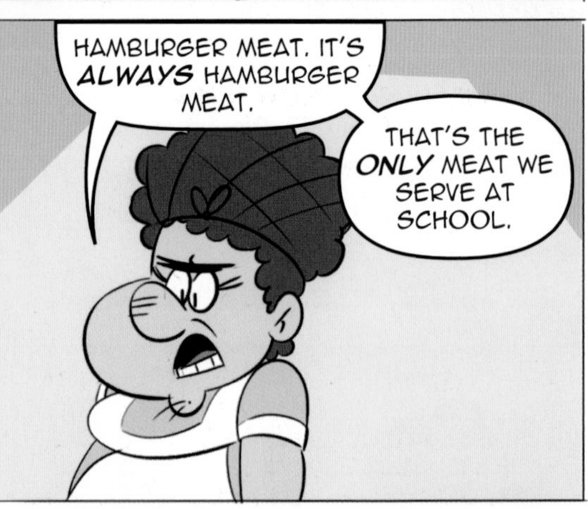
HAMBURGER MEAT. IT'S ALWAYS HAMBURGER MEAT.
THAT'S THE ONLY MEAT WE SERVE AT SCHOOL.

IF THERE'S ANYTHING I'VE LEARNED, IT'S THAT SOMETIMES THE ONLY WAY TO ENJOY THINGS...
...IS TO LEAVE THE MYSTERY UNSOLVED.
TODAY'S DESSERT ???
END?

"MODEL PETS"

LANA? ARE YOU OKAY IN THERE?
I THINK I GOT A CASE OF FOOD POISONING.
THAT'S TERRIBLE! WHAT DID YOU EAT?
NOTHING UNUSUAL. JUST SOME EXPIRED MILK MOM THREW OUT, A CAKE THAT LENI MADE FROM REAL FLOWERS INSTEAD OF FLOUR...
...OH! AND A RHUBARB. I THOUGHT IT WAS A PURPLE CELERY.
YEP, I'M PRETTY SURE IT WAS THE RHUBARB!
WORRY NOT! I KNOW A TEA RECIPE TO HELP!
Y'KNOW, LOLA, I COULD REALLY USE YOUR HELP WITH WATCHING MY PETS WHILE I'M STUCK IN BED.
I'M NOT REALLY SURE I CAN....
IF YOU CAN'T, COULD YOU DO ME A FAVOR AND UNCLOG THE TOILET?
YOU CAN EVEN BORROW BIG BERTHA.
SORRY! HOPS SAYS HE'S READY TO GO! GET BETTER SOON! BYE!

GEEZ! WHY DO I HAVE TO WATCH LANA'S GROSS PETS? I KNOW WE'RE TWINS BUT THERE IS ABSOLUTELY NOTHING CUTE ABOUT ANY OF THEM! NO OFFENSE...
RIBBIT!
WELL, LET'S GET THIS OVER WITH.
GASP!
RIB!
FLOP
SPLOTCH
SNAPPY--I MEAN BITEY... DON'T EAT THAT! NO EATING GEO, REBECCA! OR ARE YOU IZZY? UGH!

GET OFF, BRAD! MY PIT'S OFF LIMITS!
WHOOSH
AHHHHH! GROSS!
IF YOU ALL THINK I'M GOING TO STAND HERE AND WATCH THIS DISGUSTING BEHAVIOR, THINK AGAIN!
IT'S MAKE-OVER TIME!

NOW, IT IS TIME TO INTRODUCE OUR BOYS! STARRING THE NEW AND LOLA-APPROVED "HOPZ"!...
AND "EL DIA-WOAH", AND OF COURSE, MR. BRADLEY!
ED
AND DON'T FORGET THE LADIES! "IZZA THE MAGNIFICENT!" AND "BITIONIA THE BEAUTY"! AND SINCE I CAN'T REMEMBER THE REST OF YOUR NAMES..."THE GIRLS"!
SQUEAK! SQUEAK!
DON'T BE SILLY! OF COURSE YOU ARE A GIRL!
NOW THAT YOU ARE ALL PRESENTABLE! WE CAN ENJOY THE CIVILIZED TEA PARTY.

OH, HEY, LOLA! YOU'RE JUST IN TIME! SINCE YOU WERE WATCHING MY PETS I THOUGHT I'D SURPRISE YOU WITH A TEA PARTY!
I MADE MY SPECIALTY! MUD PIES!
NO! RESIST THE FILTH! RESIST IT!
HEY, GANG! I FEEL LIKE THERE'S SOME-THING DIFFERENT ABOUT YOU ALL TODAY? AM I STILL SICK?
WINK
THAT'S CAUSE I MADE THEM LOOK FABULOUS!
EVEN WITH THE MUD?
I'M JUST THAT TALENTED!
END

"DIAGNOSIS: LOUD"

AGING, AGORAPHOBIA, ALBINISM...
YES, I'M SURE MR. GROUSE HAS ALL OF THOSE THINGS, BUT THEY'RE NOT WHAT WE'RE LOOKING FOR!
WHAT DOES IT SAY ABOUT AHNENT?
NOTHING.

THIS IS FUTILE. BUT I HAVE A BACKUP PLAN.

OKAY, WELL, WE'LL JUST KEEP LOOKING FOR ANSWERS IN--
NO WAY. WHEN HAS ANYONE EVER FOUND AN ANSWER IN A BOOK?
IF MR. GROUSE'S AHNENT IS SWOLLEN, JUST LET ME DEADLIFT HIM A FEW TIMES AND IT'LL BE UNSWOLLEN!
I'M NOT SO SURE, LYNN. I REALLY THINK WE SHOULD--

YOU MAY CEASE YOUR RESEARCH, SIBLINGS!
I HAVE THE SOLUTION!
IT'S CALLED AN AHNENTOSCOPY MACHINE!

GUARANTEED TO FIX YOUR AHNENT. OR...
ANYTHING ELSE THAT MIGHT NEED FIXING.
EH?
WHAT THE HECK ARE YOU KIDS TALKIN' ABOUT?

YOUR SWOLLEN AHNENT!
SWOLLEN AHNENT?

OH...

I SAID "I SWALLOWED AN ANT!"

OH...

WELL, WE CAN HELP YOU WITH THAT!
WACK
AND AS LONG AS WE HAVE A WILLING SUBJECT, WE MIGHT AS WELL TEST THE AHNENTOSCOPY MACHINE!

NO, WAY! GET THAT MACHINE OFF MY PROPERTY RIGHT NOW!
BZZZ
GULK!

HHH-RYKK!
HRRK URK!
WELL... PRACTICE MAKES PERFECT!
END

"CAKE-ENSTEIN'S MONSTER"

CONJOINED CUPCAKES! BUT WITH VERY DIFFERENT INGREDIENTS.
VERY DIFFERENT.
YOU'D BATTER LISTEN UP WHILE I EGG-SPLAIN MY IDEAS, BECAUSE I'M GOING TO GO AT BAKE-NECK SPEED!
IS THERE AN ACTUAL REQUEST COMING, LUAN?
OR JUST THE PERFORMANCE?
SIGH. IT'S MIDNIGHT BLACK. BUT NOT, LIKE... MELANCHOLY VOID BLACK.
I'VE HAD MY AGENTS PREPARE THIS RIDER. IT OUTLINES ALL THE CUPCAKE NEEDS FOR MY GREEN ROOM.
BUT THIS IS NOT--
SIGH. IT'S FINE.
IT'S CALLED LOUDUTONIUM. IT'S NEW TO MOLECULAR GASTRONOMY.
TO SYNTHESIZE IT YOU--
POO POO.
ABSOLUTELY NOT.
BUT I MADE YOU A DOUGHNUT.

SO... YOU MADE CUPCAKES.
YES.
AND YOU--
DID NOT HEED YOUR ADVICE, AND INSTEAD TOOK INDIVIDUAL REQUESTS? YEP.
BUT ON THE VERY BRIGHT SIDE...
I HAD ENOUGH LEFTOVER BATTER TO WHIP UP A LITTLE SOMETHING SPECIAL...
...JUST FOR US.
JUST FOR YOU?

GULP
MUNCH CRUNCH
YUM!
THANKS, DAD. WE REALLY... KNEADED THIS!
BURP!
END

nickelodeon GRAPHIC NOVELS AVAILABLE FROM PAPERCUTZ

THE LOUD HOUSE
#1
"There Will Be Chaos"

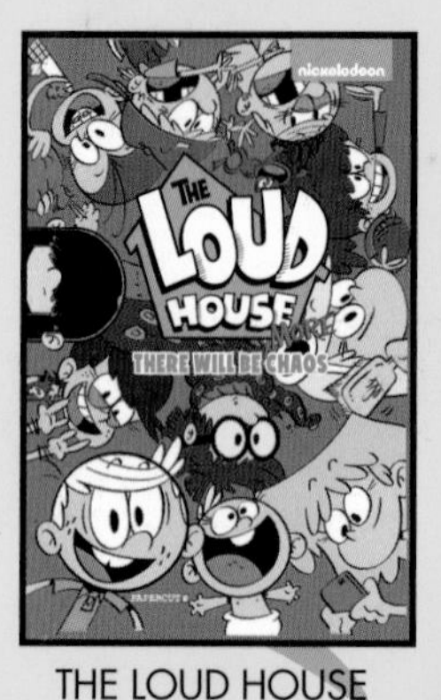

THE LOUD HOUSE
#2
"There Will Be More Chaos"

THE LOUD HOUSE
#3
"Live Life Loud!"

THE LOUD HOUSE
#4
"Family Tree"

THE LOUD HOUSE
#5
"After Dark"

THE LOUD HOUSE
#6
"Loud and Proud"

THE LOUD HOUSE
#7
"The Struggle is Real"

THE LOUD HOUSE
#8
"Livin' La Casa Loud"

THE LOUD HOUSE
#9
"Ultimate Hangout"

THE LOUD HOUSE
#10
"The Many Faces of
Lincoln Loud"

THE LOUD HOUSE
#11
"Who's the Loudest?"

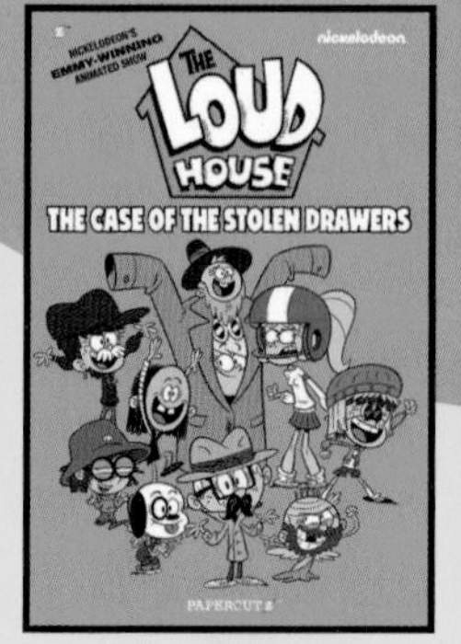

THE LOUD HOUSE
#12
"The Case of the Stolen
Drawers"

COMING SOON

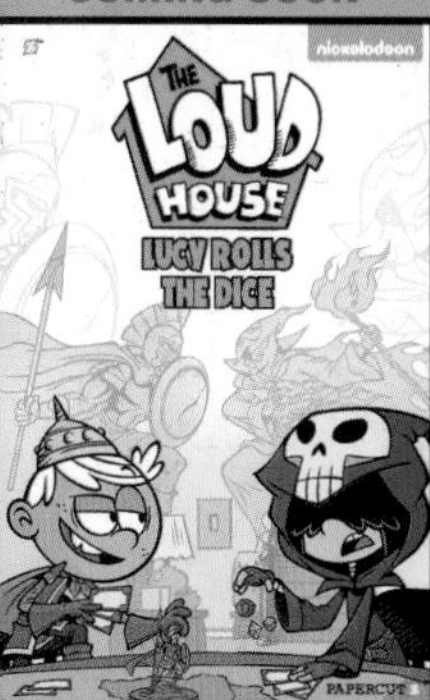

THE LOUD HOUSE
#13
"Lucy Rolls the Dice"

COMING SOON

THE LOUD HOUSE
#14
"Guessing Games"

THE LOUD HOUSE
WINTER SPECIAL

COMING SOON

THE LOUD HOUSE
SUMMER SPECIAL

THE LOUD HOUSE
3 IN 1
#1

THE LOUD HOUSE
3 IN 1
#2

THE LOUD HOUSE
3 IN 1
#3

THE CASAGRANDES
SPECIAL
#1

The Loud House and The Casagrandes graphic novels and specials are available for $7.99 each in paperback, $12.99 each in hardcover. THE LOUD HOUSE 3 IN 1 graphic novels are available for $14.99 each in paperback only. Available from booksellers everywhere. You can also order online from Papercutz.com, or call 1-800-886-1223, Monday through Friday, 9-5 EST. MC, Visa, and AmEx accepted. To order by mail, please add $5.00 for postage and handling for the first book ordered, $1.00 for each additional book and make check payable to NBM Publishing. Send to: Papercutz, 160 Broadway, Suite 700, East Wing, New York, NY 10038.

Nickelodeon graphic novels are also available digitally wherever e-books are sold.

WATCH OUT FOR PAPERCUTZ

Welcome to the fearsome ("The Haunted House," "Cake-nstein's Monster," "Candy Hunting at Huntington Manor," "Macabre Munchies," etc.) and fashionable ("Model Bahavior," "Model Pets," etc.) fourth THE LOUD HOUSE 3 IN 1 graphic novel from Papercutz—those parenthesis-loving people dedicated to publishing great graphic novels for all ages. I'm Jim Salicrup, Editor-in-Chief and Last Page Sage here to re-assure you that though this may be the last page of this particular THE LOUD HOUSE graphic novel, there's still plenty of the Loud family, and their friends the Casagrandes coming to keep you entertained in these crazy times, and we're not just talking about their hit shows on Nickelodeon...

First off, there's THE LOUD HOUSE SUMMER SPECIAL. Summer truly is special. School's out and there's plenty of time for fun. Not that the Loud family doesn't have fun all year round, but if you live somewhere where it snows in the winter, those hot summer beach days are precious. So, Lincoln and his sisters Lori, Leni, Luna, Lynn, Luan, Lucy (yes, even Lucy!), Lola, Lana, and Lily can't wait to hit the beach or chill out by the pool, or just look for a delicious icy treat to beat the heat. The Casagrandes are included in the fun as well. Ronnie Anne, Bobby, and the rest of their extended family are searching for foolproof ways of handling the scorching summer in the big city. This extra-special graphic novel features a mix of new stories and past favorites from THE LOUD HOUSE graphic novel series.

And speaking of Ronnie Anne's family, guess who are about to star in their very own graphic novel? That's right! Papercutz presents the very first THE CASAGRANDES graphic novel, based on the show of the same name spinning off from THE LOUD HOUSE that's all about the culture, humor and love of growing up in a multi-generational Mexican-American family. When Lincoln Loud's good friend Ronnie Anne, her brother Bobby, and their mother Maria, moved away from Royal Woods to Great Lakes City, it was a big change. Now they're enjoying life with their *abuelos* (grandparents) Hector and Rosa, plus Rosa's brother Carlos, his wife Frida, and their four kids — Carlota, CJ, Carl, and Carlitos — not to mention their pets, Lalo the dog and Sergio the bird. It's all just one big happy family living above Hector and Rosa's *mercado* in the big city! This special features both new stories and past favorites which appeared in THE LOUD HOUSE graphic novels. Plus as an extra-special bonus we're featuring three exclusive mini-interviews with a few of the real live talents behind the animated show *The Casagrandes*. You'll get to meet Co-Executive Producer Miguel Puga, Consulting Producer and Cultural Consultant Lalo Alcaraz, and the voice of Ronnie Anne, Izabella Alvarez!

And if those two graphic novels can't satisfy your cravings for more of THE LOUD HOUSE, don't worry. Coming soon is the all-new THE LOUD HOUSE #13 "Lucy Rolls the Dice"! Find out what happens when a storm knocks out the electricity at the Loud House and the kids have to find new ways to entertain themselves. With these ten kids we're sure they'll come up with a few surprises.

Thanks,

STAY IN TOUCH!

EMAIL:	salicrup@papercutz.com
WEB:	papercutz.com
TWITTER:	@papercutzgn
INSTAGRAM:	@papercutzgn
FACEBOOK:	PAPERCUTZGRAPHICNOVELS
FANMAIL:	Papercutz, 160 Broadway, Suite 700, East Wing, New York, NY 10038

Go to papercutz.com and sign up for the free Papercutz e-newsletter!